"Your being here is slowly driving me insane."

She swallowed. "That certainly isn't my intention."

"Of course not." He set his now half-empty bottle beside hers on the counter and took a step closer... gently cupped her face in his hands, started to lower his head.

Her breath caught in her throat. His intent was obvious, and although a part of her desperately yearned to feel his mouth on hers, another part screamed at her to step away, out of temptation's reach. She fisted her hands, her nails biting into her palms. "Don't kiss me, Nick."

"Why not?"

"Because." She swallowed. "Because it would be a mistake."

"Probably," he agreed, his lips whispering against her cheek. "And it's a mistake I can't stop myself from making."

Dear Reader,

Most of us look forward to October for the end-of-the-month treats, but we here at Silhouette Special Edition want you to experience those treats all month long—beginning, this time around, with the next book in our MOST LIKELY TO… series. In *The Pregnancy Project* by Victoria Pade, a woman who's used to getting what she wants, wants a baby. And the man she's earmarked to help her is her arrogant ex-classmate, now a brilliant, if brash, fertility expert.

Popular author Gina Wilkins brings back her acclaimed FAMILY FOUND series with *Adding to the Family,* in which a party girl turned single mother of twins needs help—and her handsome accountant *(accountant?),* a single father himself, is just the one to give it. In *She's Having a Baby,* bestselling author Marie Ferrarella continues her miniseries, THE CAMEO, with this story of a vivacious, single, pregnant woman and her devastatingly handsome—if reserved—next-door neighbor. Special Edition welcomes author Brenda Harlen and her poignant novel *Once and Again,* a heartwarming story of homecoming and second chances. *About the Boy* by Sharon DeVita is the story of a beautiful single mother, a widowed chief of police…and a matchmaking little boy. And Silhouette is thrilled to have *Blindsided* by talented author Leslie LaFoy in our lineup. When a woman who's inherited a hockey team decides that they need the best coach in the business, she applies to a man who thought he'd put his hockey days behind him. But he's been…blindsided!

So enjoy, be safe and come back in November for more. This is my favorite time of year (well, the beginning of it, anyway).

Regards,

Gail Chasan
Senior Editor

Please address questions and book requests to:
Silhouette Reader Service
U.S.: 3010 Walden Ave., P.O. Box 1325, Buffalo, NY 14269
Canadian: P.O. Box 609, Fort Erie, Ont. L2A 5X3

ONCE *and* AGAIN
BRENDA HARLEN

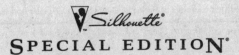

SPECIAL EDITION

Published by Silhouette Books

America's Publisher of Contemporary Romance

Thanks to Stephanie McCarragher, R.N., for all the medical info—
and more. The good stuff is all hers, any errors are my own. To
Gail Chasan, for giving me this chance. And to Linda Kruger,
a wonderful woman, an incredible agent and a terrific friend.
I will always be grateful for the opportunity and
privilege of working with you. You're the best!

 SILHOUETTE BOOKS

ISBN 0-373-24714-1

ONCE AND AGAIN

Copyright © 2005 by Brenda Harlen

BRENDA HARLEN

grew up in a small town surrounded by books and imaginary friends. Although she always dreamed of being a writer, she chose to follow a more traditional career path first. After two years of practicing as an attorney (including an appearance in front of the Supreme Court of Canada), she gave up her "real" job to be a mom and to try her hand at writing books. Three years, five manuscripts and another baby later, she sold her first book—an RWA Golden Heart winner—to Silhouette.

Brenda lives in southern Ontario with her real-life husband/hero, two heroes-in-training and two neurotic dogs. She is still surrounded by books ("too many books," according to her children) and imaginary friends, but she also enjoys communicating with "real" people. Readers can contact Brenda by e-mail at brendaharlen@yahoo.com or by snail mail c/o Silhouette Books, 233 Broadway, Suite 1001, New York, NY 10279.

September 22

Dear Nick,

It's been a year since you walked out of my life without so much as a backward glance. I still don't know why things ended the way they did, what happened to sever the ties between us so completely. And I'm not sure why I'm writing this letter now, when I probably won't ever find the courage to send it. But I need you to know that I'm sorry for everything, and I wish we could somehow find a way to bridge the distance that has grown between us, to forgive the pain we've caused one another. Maybe that's too much to ask after everything that's happened, but I can't give up hope that someday we might make it happen. That maybe we could even be friends again....

Prologue

It was a dream come true for any seven-year-old boy.

In fact, the gleaming red-and-silver bicycle was exactly what Caleb had been dreaming about for weeks. Every time his mom took him downtown, he'd tug on her hand and drag her over to the window of Beckett's Sporting Goods store to look at it—just one more time.

Now, thanks to Aunt Jessica, it was his.

He wrapped his fingers around the black rubber grips, threw one leg over the crossbar, settled his foot on the pedal, pushed off with the other. His friends hovered on the edge of the driveway, watching with a combination of envious excitement and eager anticipation that he might give them each a turn.

He sailed down the driveway, grinning at the wind in his face, then turned sharply at the bottom and pumped his legs to climb up again. This was so much better than the scratched and dented hand-me-down of Jake's he used to ride.

"Are we gonna have cake now, Mom?"

He threw the question over his shoulder as he zipped past her again.

"Whenever you're ready," she said.

"Cake," his friends chanted in unison.

She smiled and turned toward the house.

She didn't actually see what happened next, but she heard it. She would never forget the sounds.

The squeal of tires.

The crunch of metal.

The sickening thud.

And sudden, deafening silence.

Then came the screams.

And finally, the piercing wail of sirens.

Chapter One

Eighteen years ago, Jessica Harding couldn't wait to leave Pinehurst, New York. She'd had plans for her life—plans that were bigger than this small town. Shortly after high school graduation, immediately after Kristin and Brian's wedding, she'd packed her meager belongings into her rusty secondhand car and headed for New York City.

Now she was back.

She paid little attention to the familiar landmarks as she ignored the speed limit on her way toward the hospital. She could think only of her best friend's youngest child and the birthday celebration that had ended in tragedy.

Jess had declined the invitation to Caleb's party, sending her gift along with her regrets that she wouldn't be able to attend.

But she'd had no regrets.

Until now.

Now, as she turned into the visitor parking lot, she was filled with them.

Mostly she regretted that she hadn't chosen another gift.

But she knew less than nothing about the interests of a seven-year-old boy, and when she'd heard Caleb had been admiring a certain bicycle in the front window of Beckett's Sporting Goods store, it had seemed the easy answer.

She'd never anticipated that her gift might bring tragedy to her best friend's family.

Stepping out of her BMW, she heard the chime of bells in the distance, summoning parishioners to worship. Holy Trinity, she guessed, on the corner of the next block. Which meant it was almost eleven-thirty.

She glanced at her watch.

Some things never changed.

And some, of course, did.

She hurried up the concrete sidewalk toward the sliding glass doors at the main entrance and wondered if she'd recognize Caleb when she saw him. She tried to recall the details of the most recent photos Kristin had sent, but in her mind, he was still the chubby-cheeked toddler on unsteady legs she'd met on her last visit home. That was the picture that came to mind, the mental image that refused to fade.

He'd been such a beautiful child, with Kristin's soft blond curls and sparkling blue eyes, and—even at ten months—a devilish grin. And when he'd crawled into her lap to lay his head on her shoulder, rubbing his weary eyes with his dimpled little fists, Jessica's heart had simply melted.

Until that moment, she hadn't let herself think too much about all that she'd lost or the opportunities she would never have. Instead, she'd focused almost exclusively on her career, working upwards of eighty hours a week as a corporate attorney at Dawson, Murray & Neale. She'd earned the designer wardrobe, the expensive sports car and the executive condo overlooking Central Park. And yet, the moment she'd wrapped her arms around her best friend's youngest child, she'd realized how empty her life was.

Six months later, determined to fill the void, she'd married Steve Garrison, another lawyer at the firm. Although they both had ambitions of making partner, she'd been happy to focus her immediate attention on the family they both wanted. But despite their best efforts, Jess had been unable to conceive. Three childless years later, Steve—now a partner—had walked out, leaving her with only client files and time sheets to keep her company during the long nights made lonelier by the acceptance that she would never hold a child of her own in her arms.

But Jess didn't let herself dwell on that now. She was here to support Kristin and Brian, to help ease their grief— and her own guilt.

She'd always envied Kristin and Brian—the forever kind of love they shared, the family they'd made. Even back in high school, everyone had known they would end up together. The football star and the head cheerleader, they'd been perfect for one another, perfect together.

Yes, Jess had envied them.

But not now.

After a quick stop at the information desk to inquire about Caleb's room number, she made her way down the main corridor, the heels of her shoes clicking a staccato rhythm on the granite tile. She passed a couple of nurses hurrying in the opposite direction and noted that instead

of the usual mint green hospital scrubs, they both wore blue
pants and tunics covered with teddy bears. Obviously the
attire was intended to appeal to the children who were pa-
tients here, but it seemed to Jess patently unfair that there
needed to be an entire wing of the hospital devoted to children's illnesses and injuries.

She felt the sting of tears as she thought of Caleb, and
the sharper pang of regret that hadn't subsided since she'd
learned of his accident.

Guilt and grief weren't new emotions to Jess. They were
the reason—or at least one of the reasons—she'd been ab-
sent from this town for so long.

She turned the corner toward the bank of elevators and
came face-to-face with another of the reasons she'd stayed
away: Nick.

Throughout most of the three-hour drive, Jess had been
preoccupied with thoughts of Caleb and Kristin and Brian. Even so, in the back of her mind, she'd known it was
inevitable that she'd run into Nick. But she'd thought she'd
have time to prepare for their eventual meeting, time to
plan how she'd handle the situation, time to prepare herself for the inevitable battering of her heart.

But there had been no time, no planning, no preparation.
He was suddenly just there. Standing in front of the elevator, as devastatingly handsome as she remembered.

Oh, there were subtle signs of the passing of time: a few
strands of silver mixed in with the blond hair at his tem-
ples, the fanning of lines from the corner of his eyes. But
his eyes were the same dreamy shade of blue, the line of
his jaw still square and strong, the curve of his lips still boy-
ishly charming.

Except that when he glanced up at her, those dreamy

eyes were as cold as shards of ice and the curve of his lips thinned into a disapproving line.

Jessica straightened her spine, held her head up. She didn't need or want anyone's approval—least of all Nick Armstrong's.

After years of being friends and a brief interlude as lovers, their lives had taken them in decidedly different directions. Or maybe they'd deliberately set off in those directions, putting as much time and distance as possible between them, as if doing so could leave the heartbreak behind.

It hadn't worked.

At least not for Jessica.

But she'd gone on, she'd endured. She'd built a life for herself, a career she was proud of. And yet, with one scathing look, he'd managed to strip away all sense of accomplishment, leaving her empty and aching, yearning for something that had never really been, could never be again.

But she'd be damned before she'd let him know it.

"Hello, Nick." She was pleased that when she spoke, her voice was coolly neutral.

He punched the already illuminated elevator call button. "What are you doing here, Jessica?"

She twisted the strap of her purse around her hand. "I came to see Caleb. And Kristin."

"Well, you should have saved yourself the trip," Nick said coldly. "Kristin doesn't need you here."

"I want to help."

"She has her family if she needs anything. Me, Brian, and Jake and Katie."

"I can help with Jake and Katie. I can get them ready for school and—"

He laughed, shortly, derisively. "They're teenagers," he

told her. "They don't need any help getting dressed in the morning. They can make their own breakfast if they want it. And they know how to tell time to be outside waiting when the bus comes."

His scornful dismissal was another well-aimed blow, but Jessica wasn't going to give him the satisfaction of acknowledging it. She tilted her chin. "I'm not going to leave."

The elevator signaled its arrival.

Nick stepped through the open doors. "Yes, you will."

It wasn't just the words, but the smug arrogance of his tone. She resented the accusation. More, she resented the truth in it. Her fingers gripped her purse strap tighter as she followed him into the car, moving to the opposite side.

"I have a life in New York," she reminded him coolly. "Am I supposed to apologize for that?"

"No." He punched the button for the fourth floor. "So long as you go back to it."

Jessica swallowed around the uncomfortable tightness in her throat. Dammit, she hadn't come here for this. She didn't need his antagonism, but maybe she deserved it. Maybe it was finally time to clear the air between them.

"Why does it matter to you, Nick? Why do you care whether I'm here or there or on the other side of the world?"

It was a challenge—an opportunity for them to finally talk about what had happened the night Kristin and Brian got married, and what had happened after.

But he didn't respond to her challenge. He didn't say anything about their tumultuous history or what—if anything—that night had meant to him. In fact, he didn't say anything at all for a long moment.

"Why do I care?" He repeated her question, considered.

She held her breath, waiting for his response.

The elevator doors slid open.

He shrugged. "I guess I don't."

Nick saw the flicker of hurt in her eyes, the hint of sadness in the whiskey-colored depths, before she turned away and stepped out of the elevator.

He bit back a sigh of regret, knowing his response had been unnecessarily harsh, needlessly cruel. It had also been untrue.

The truth was, he cared a whole hell of a lot.

Maybe too much.

And seeing Jessica again, after so many years, with so many things still unsettled between them, made him a little irrational. There was something about Jessica that had always made him crazy.

He sighed inwardly. The fact that she still did was his own problem, and one he would need to deal with so long as she was in Pinehurst. Which, he reassured himself, wouldn't be very long.

Seeing Jessica had distracted him from his original purpose—to check on Caleb. Then again, Jessica had always been something of a distraction.

As a kid, he'd thought of her as Kristin's pesky friend, a solemn child who'd followed him around asking questions about anything and everything. By the time she was fourteen, she'd become a distraction of an entirely different kind, with curves that other girls envied and teenage boys lusted for. He'd been a perfectly normal teenage boy, which created something of a moral dilemma for Nick and made him all the more anxious to go off to architectural college and escape his prurient desires.

And it had worked—at least for a while.

But he was an adult now, not a hormonal teenager, and while there was still something about Jessica that got to him on a basic level, he wasn't about to let it distract him.

Jess stopped in the middle of the hallway, so abruptly he nearly ran into her. He wasn't sure if her hesitation was because she didn't know where she was going or because she was unsure what she would find when she walked into Caleb's hospital room.

Or maybe she was just having second thoughts about being anywhere in his company.

It had been that way for the past eighteen years—as soon as one of them entered a room, the other would leave. He didn't think it was obvious to anyone else, especially since their paths had crossed only a half dozen times during that period. But it was obvious to him, and he knew it was his fault.

Maybe if he'd been able to get past his own hurt and anger to let her explain why she'd made the choices she had, there wouldn't be this painful awkwardness between them now. Or maybe he was deluding himself. Maybe there was simply no way to get back to that place where they could be friends, not after they'd been lovers.

"Room 426," he said gruffly.

"I know." She turned to him with obvious reluctance, her even white teeth sinking into the soft fullness of her bottom lip. His gaze dipped automatically, lingered.

So much for not letting her distract him.

"I just wanted to know…" She hesitated. "Jake wasn't able to tell me much about…Caleb's condition. He only said that he'd been hit…by a car."

Her golden eyes pleaded softly.

He felt his resolve weaken.

"He was knocked out initially but regained consciousness by the time the paramedics arrived. At first he was lucid, but they admitted him as a precaution, to continue to observe his condition.

"Late last night he had a seizure, and then another one this morning. Now he's lapsed into a coma."

She flinched.

He'd had the same reaction when he'd first heard the news. One little word—four seemingly innocuous letters—that had the power to destroy his sister's family.

"He rode off the end of the driveway, into the street, right in front of Harold Lansky's car. Mr. Lansky wasn't driving very fast, and the doctors say that, along with the fact that Caleb was wearing a helmet, probably saved his life."

She drew in a deep breath and nodded for him to continue.

"Still, they suspect that the force of the impact when he hit the windshield bruised his brain."

"Have they considered sending him to Midtown Children's Hospital?"

He bristled at the question. "This is one of the best hospitals in the country—even if it isn't in New York City."

"But Dr. Reid—one of the best neurosurgeons in the world—is at MCH. I had a client whose ten-year-old daughter had a brain aneurysm," she explained. "He did the surgery."

"Do me a favor," he said. "Don't mention that to Kristin."

"Why not?" She sounded genuinely baffled.

"Because I don't think she'd be thrilled about the idea of any doctor, regardless of his reputation, poking around in her son's brain."

She blinked, obviously startled by his vehement response. "I'm sorry," she said softly.

"Yeah, well being sorry doesn't always cut it." He heard the bitterness and resentment he'd tried so hard to control, knew she couldn't have missed it.

"Are we still talking about Caleb?"

"Right now, he's the only thing that matters."

She nodded. "Then maybe we could shelve the hostility for a while?"

Nick shrugged again, as if her sudden and unexpected appearance here didn't bother him. As if her proximity didn't stir within him the familiar battling forces of hatred and longing.

He hated that she'd walked away from him without a backward glance when he would have gone anywhere with her. He hated that she'd chosen her career over their relationship when he would have done anything for her. And he hated that, after eighteen years, he still wanted her.

Even when he looked at her now—the long dark hair he remembered cut stylishly short, the soft, luscious curves that still haunted his dreams elegantly covered by a silky top and slightly rumpled linen trousers—all he could think about was peeling away those layers of polish and pretense to reveal the uninhibited passion of the woman inside.

Except there was no hint of that passion in the gaze that met his own, only a silent plea he cursed himself for being unable to ignore.

"Consider it shelved," he said.

Her smile was brief, tentative. Still it stirred something inside him. Something he didn't want stirred.

He followed her reluctantly into Caleb's room, wishing that she'd go back to New York.

* * *

If it hadn't been for the fact that Nick was right on her heels, Jess might very well have hesitated again. She was nervous, uncertain of the reception she would receive after being away for so long. Uncertain of so many things when it came to the woman who had always been her best friend. But she walked briskly into the room, refusing to give Nick even a glimpse of the doubts that plagued her.

Kristin was perched on the edge of a narrow mattress, one leg tucked beneath her, both hands cradling one of her child's much smaller ones.

Jess battled against the feeling of helplessness that threatened to overwhelm her as she searched for something to say.

It was Kristin who spoke first, her eyes widening when she saw her old friend standing there.

"Jessica?" It was a question more than a greeting.

Still, it propelled her forward, and she moved to embrace her friend. "I came as soon as I could."

Kristin, still apparently baffled by her presence, sent a quick glance at her brother, as if Nick might have the answers she sought. "But why—how did you know?"

"I called this morning…" She swallowed around the lump in her throat. "I caught Jake at home…he said he was on his way to the hospital…he told me about the accident."

"He never mentioned that he spoke to you," she said. Then she turned to Nick again, her voice carrying an edge of panic as she asked, "Where is Jake? And Katie?"

Nick rubbed a hand over Kristin's back. "Jake had to work," he reminded her. "I dropped him off at the grocery store and convinced Katie to take in a movie with Allison."

"Oh, right." She nodded. "Okay. Thanks."

"No problem."

While Kristin and Nick were talking, Jessica turned her attention to Caleb. She was shocked at how pale and still and silent he was. Pale, except for the raw scrapes across his cheek and on his chin. Still, except for the slow and steady rise and fall of his chest controlled by the tube down his throat. Silent, except for the rhythmic hisses and beeps of the machines attached to his tiny body.

She reached over to brush her fingers gently over the curve of his paper-white cheek. His skin was soft, cool to the touch. "You sure have grown since the last time I saw you," she murmured.

"It's been six years," Kristin said tonelessly.

It wasn't a reprimand or recrimination, just a statement of fact. Jess only nodded. "I'm so sorry, Kristin."

"So am I—but that doesn't help my son at all."

Jess flinched again, even though she knew there was nothing she could say or do to make Kristin feel any better. There was nothing anyone could do to ease the inexplicable pain and anger and frustration her friend was enduring.

Nick moved away from his sister to settle into a chair on the other side of Caleb's bed, but Jess felt his eyes on her.

"I didn't mean to snap at you," Kristin said after a moment of awkward silence. "I'm just not in the mood for a joyful reunion right now."

"That's not why I came."

"Why did you come?"

"I thought you could use a friend," she said softly.

Kristin stared at her for a long moment, her eyes filled with sadness, before finally saying, "Yeah, I probably could."

The lack of enthusiasm didn't surprise Jessica. After almost two decades, she shouldn't have expected they would immediately fall into old habits and patterns. They'd kept in touch, but occasional letters and infrequent phone calls weren't enough to sustain the bond they'd once shared. Especially when most of those letters and calls originated in Pinehurst. It was just one more thing Jessica regretted.

Kristin had tried so many times to get her to come back, but Jessica had always refused. She'd offered one excuse after another, but in the end, they were still just excuses.

She'd taken the easy way out: avoiding her friend and staying away from Pinehurst to ensure she wouldn't run into Nick.

It hadn't been easy, but it had been easier.

Easier to walk away than to risk all her hopes and dreams on a man who didn't share her feelings. Easier to stay away than to let her best friend know that she'd fallen in love with her brother.

It was the first secret she'd ever kept from Kristin. The first, but not the last. Now there was so much they didn't know about one another. And Jess couldn't help but wonder if her sudden appearance only made a difficult situation even more difficult for her friend.

"I want to be here for you," she said softly. "But I won't stay if you don't want me to."

Kristin was silent for another long moment before saying, "I'm just surprised that you came."

The simple honesty of the statement struck a sharper blow than any angry words or accusations possibly could.

Then silence descended again, awkward and all-encompassing.

It was all wrong—their whole interaction was like a

badly choreographed play, as if they'd studied their lines but didn't know how to act. They were saying the right things, and yet there was something missing. Something Jessica couldn't define, but the absence of which made her feel incredibly sad.

"Where were you planning to stay?" Kristin finally asked.

"I'll probably get a room at the hotel," she said.

There was another hesitation, and another long moment passed, before Kristin said, "There's a pullout sofa in our den."

Then she shrugged, and Jessica knew she was waiting for her to decline the offer. As she'd declined so many offers in the past.

"I don't know how comfortable it is," she continued. "But it's there. Or maybe Nick—"

"The sofa sounds perfect," Jessica interrupted quickly.

Kristin seemed surprised by her quick acceptance, but then she managed a hesitant smile. "I'll give you my key."

Chapter Two

As Jess negotiated the familiar roads on her way to Kristin and Brian's house, she was amazed by how little had changed through the years. When she'd traveled this same route a couple hours earlier, she'd been too intent on getting to the hospital to register any of the surroundings. Now that she'd seen Kristin and knew Caleb's condition was—although still critical—at least stable, she was able to get a better impression of the town she'd grown up in.

Anderson's Hardware was still on the corner of Main and Wilson Streets, next to Time & Again—a secondhand store—and The Book Market.

The cybercafé was new.

That café had been a pizza parlor when Jessica was in high school, and she'd worked there after school and on weekends. She'd been working the day Nick Armstrong had come home after his first year away at college, and when he'd walked into the restaurant her sixteen-year-old heart had tripped and fallen at his feet.

Nick had been her first crush. Her first lover. Her first heartbreak.

She pushed away those thoughts as she braked for a red light, coming to a stop beside Brody's Drugstore. The front window was decorated for Halloween even though it was only the middle of September. The seasons seemed to slip past so quickly now—as her life seemed to be doing. She sighed as she continued her perusal. Across the street was Emma's Flower Shop, with bouquets of fresh-cut flowers out front to tempt passersby; beside the florist was Beckett's Sporting Goods store, advertising a storewide clearance on Rollerblades, skateboards and bicycles.

She felt the sting of tears again. Would Kristin ever be able to forgive her?

Would she ever forgive herself?

She pulled into the driveway and wondered if she'd made a mistake in coming back.

When she'd heard about Caleb's accident, she'd paused only long enough to throw a few things in a suitcase. Now, as she carried that suitcase to the house, she started to doubt the wisdom of her impulsive actions. Not just because of the unplanned meeting with Nick and the unwelcome onslaught of memories, but because of the unexpected distance between her and Kristin that she didn't know how to bridge.

She should have expected that there would be some awkwardness between them. It was naive to hope that the bonds between them would have endured despite the passing of time. But it was what she'd hoped, and she'd been foolishly disappointed to find otherwise.

Jess had been seven—the same age Caleb was now—when she'd moved to Pinehurst. She'd met Kristin on her first day in Mrs. Hartwick's second-grade class at Parkdale Elementary School. From that day on, they'd been the best of friends.

Kristin and Jessica. Jessica and Kristin.

Her mom used to tease that where one went, the other would follow. But that wasn't really an accurate description of their relationship. They were partners, allies, equals.

They used to talk for hours on the phone every night, discussing homework assignments, comparing notes on boys and making plans for the future. Top of their list was to get out of Pinehurst and see the world together.

Then Kristin had fallen in love, and instead of pursuing her dream of going off to college, she'd chosen to stay in Pinehurst to marry Brian Clarke. And Jess, more determined than ever to follow her own path, had taken her scholarship to Columbia University and gone to New York City alone.

Eighteen years later, Kristin was still happily married to her high school sweetheart, living in the home where she'd grown up and the mother of three beautiful children. Jessica had a successful career as a corporate attorney, an apartment with a great view and absolutely nothing else.

They were adults now, with adult lives and responsibilities, and not just geography but a lot of history separating them.

Still, she was optimistic that they could bridge that distance one step at a time. The first step, and the most difficult for Jess, had been coming home. Now that she was here, she was determined to do what she could to help her oldest friend.

She unlocked the door and stepped inside.

As a child, she'd spent almost as much time in this house as in her own. And although Kristin and Brian had made some minor changes after Kristin's mom had passed away—walls painted, appliances updated, furniture replaced—those changes didn't detract at all from the sense of homecoming.

She shook her head, surprised by her feelings of nostalgia. When she'd left Pinehurst, she'd willingly left all of this behind. Now that she was back, she couldn't remember why she'd been so anxious to go.

She moved through the archway and into the dining room, her heart breaking a little to see the remnants of Caleb's birthday party. There were still blue and orange streamers hanging from the ceiling and bouquets of now deflated helium balloons in the corners. The long table was covered with a paper cloth that bore traces of macaroni salad and potato chip crumbs. A half-empty punch bowl, bottles of ketchup and mustard and an open jar of relish were further remnants of the feast. Napkins had been scrunched up and discarded along with plastic cutlery.

She picked up a cone-shaped party hat, traced her fingers over the glittering letters that spelled out "Happy Birthday" across the front. The fist that had gripped her heart since she'd learned of the accident squeezed tighter.

She closed her eyes but couldn't banish the image of Caleb in that hospital bed with a ventilator to breathe for him, tubes to feed him, and machines monitoring every function of his body.

She'd taken one look at him and had been almost overwhelmed by fear and guilt. She wanted to support Kristin, to be the friend she hadn't been for so long, but maybe too much time had passed. Maybe it really was too late.

What good could she do anyway? She wasn't a doctor or a psychologist or even a social worker. She was a lawyer—a corporate attorney who'd buried herself in her job for ten years because it was the one thing she knew she was good at. And a woman who, as much as she hated to admit it, had abandoned her best friend a long time ago.

Standing here now, in Kristin's dining room, she knew she'd made a mistake in coming back. She couldn't help her friend, and there was almost nothing she hated more than feeling helpless.

She turned to leave, and then she saw it.

On the sideboard.

An uncut birthday cake with seven unlit candles.

R2-D2. She recognized the droid character immediately and realized the recent resurgence of *Star Wars* popularity must have hooked Kristin's youngest son, as it had hooked her and Kristin when they were young.

The cake was perfect in both shape and color, with the tiniest details painstakingly recreated. She knew immediately that Kristin had made it. The degree of care and attention evident in the finished product could never be bought, but was an obvious reflection of a mother's love.

It was this uncut cake, this visual reminder of a celebration cut short by tragedy, that was nearly her undoing.

Emotions churned inside her, clamored for release. Jess held them back. Suppressing her feelings was another thing she'd always been good at. Tears were a luxury she couldn't afford right now and crying wouldn't make any difference. Not to Kristin or Brian, and certainly not to Caleb.

Jess looked around once more. Cleaning up this mess couldn't possibly ease her friend's burden, but at least it was something useful she could do.

She returned to the kitchen to find a garbage bag.

"I wasn't sure if you'd still be here."

She hadn't heard the door, and when his voice broke the silence, she started, her heart in her throat, her pulse racing wildly. Turning, she found herself once again face-to-face with Nick, and no more prepared for this meeting than she'd been for their earlier encounter.

She exhaled slowly, her heart receding to its appropriate location, her pulse continuing to beat just a little too fast. "I told you I wasn't going anywhere."

"Yeah, that's what you said," he agreed.

"Then you shouldn't be surprised by my presence." She turned and headed back to the dining room.

Of course, he followed.

There had been a time when she'd wanted more than anything to be with him, and he'd walked out on her. Now, when she wanted only to be alone, she couldn't get rid of him.

"Why are *you* here, Nick?"

It was the same question he'd asked himself on the way over. The answer, he knew, was simple—because he wasn't smart enough to stay away. It wasn't an answer he was going to share with Jessica, though.

"I thought I'd come by to clean up."

"I can take care of it."

"I'm sure you can." He bent to pick up a crumpled piece of discarded wrapping paper. "But it will go quicker if we work together."

"Work together?" she echoed, as if it were a completely foreign concept.

Not that he could blame her for being suspicious. After so many years of distance and silence, why would she expect that he'd want to do anything with her? But despite that nothing had changed between them, he could appreciate that she was trying to help and show that appreciation by making an effort to be civil.

"You were the one who suggested shelving the hostility," he reminded her. "I thought we could take that a step further and, if not actually cooperate, at least coexist for the short term." He shoved a handful of crepe streamers into the bag she carried and couldn't help adding, "That is, if you're determined to hang around."

Her eyes narrowed, shooting molten sparks of gold. "I'm staying."

Then she bent over the table to roll up the paper cloth with the disposable partyware inside.

He watched her, noting that her chic, short haircut exposed the graceful line of her neck and the deep vee of her sleeveless top revealed just the slightest hint of cleavage as she bent over the table. His gaze drifted downward, to the narrow waist, slender hips and endlessly long legs. Her feet, he noticed, were bare, and her toenails painted a vibrant shade of red.

Damn, she was still a distraction.

Nick, determined not to let himself be distracted, turned his attention elsewhere.

"No!"

Jessica's vehement protest startled him, and she took advantage of his pause to grab the cake board from his hands.

He caught a whiff of her perfume as she pulled back, something light and spicy that called to the baser parts of his anatomy. It was different than the scent she'd worn so many years before. Then again, a lot of things were different now. And yet, so much had stayed the same—including his body's instinctive response to her nearness.

He stared at her, at the flush of color that infused her cheeks as she clutched the cake protectively against her chest. The fierce, almost desperate determination in her golden eyes sparked a long-forgotten memory.

Not forgotten really, but buried. And as a hint of that memory started to surface, he remembered *why* it was buried. Why it was best to leave it that way.

"Kristin made this," she said, as though it explained everything.

"There's no reason to keep it."

"There's every reason."

"It's an unnecessary reminder of a tragic day."

A day he knew he wouldn't ever forget.

Although he was trying to maintain a positive outlook, especially for his sister's sake, doubts were starting to creep in. He knew it was possible, although it was a possibility he didn't want to consider, that Caleb might be suffering from a serious brain injury. And with every hour that Caleb remained in the coma, the outlook grew dimmer.

He loved all of Kristin's kids, but he felt a special connection to Caleb. Maybe because he knew that his sister's third pregnancy was unplanned, and he'd wanted to ensure that his youngest nephew never felt unwanted. Maybe because Caleb had been born when his own marriage had started to fall apart, and he wanted to fill the void in his own life that came from accepting he wasn't likely to ever have any children of his own.

"It's not a reminder of a tragedy," she denied, interrupting his thoughts. "It's a symbol of a celebration unfinished. And when Caleb wakes up, he's going to want this cake."

Nick wasn't convinced Caleb would want any reminders of this day, but the strength of her conviction dissuaded further argument. He shrugged, as if it didn't matter. As if her absolute confidence in Caleb's recovery hadn't touched a dark place in his heart that desperately needed the light of reassurance.

"Then do something with it," he said gruffly. "So Kristin doesn't have to see it when she comes home."

Jessica carried it to the kitchen.

It's just a cake, Nick assured himself. There was absolutely no reason to believe that she had any residual power over him because he relented on this one issue.

But his gaze lingered on the doorway through which she'd disappeared.

Jessica was washing up the few dishes in the sink when Nick came back through the kitchen. Now that most of the cleanup was finished, she expected that he would make an excuse and be on his way. Instead, he took the carafe from the coffeemaker and brought it over to the sink to fill it with water.

His hand brushed against her arm as he reached for the tap. The contact was obviously accidental, as his hastily mumbled apology attested, and yet the fleeting contact stirred unwelcome memories, unwanted yearnings.

She wiped a soapy sponge around the inside of a bowl and fought back the unexpected sting of tears. This was exactly why she'd stayed away for so long. Because being with Nick inevitably made her feel things she didn't want to feel, want things she'd always known she could never have.

Still, she hadn't expected the pain to be so raw, the longing so intense. It had been eighteen years, and yet she still couldn't forget how it felt to be in his arms. She couldn't forget the hopes and dreams they'd briefly shared. And she couldn't forget, had never forgotten, the overwhelming emptiness that had nearly consumed her when all of those hopes and dreams had fallen apart.

He measured coffee grounds into the filter as Jessica fought to get her emotions under control. She was more tempted than she wanted to admit to get into her car and head back to New York. And maybe she would have, except she refused to give him the satisfaction of doing what he so obviously expected.

After he'd set the coffee to perk, he picked up a tea towel and began drying the dishes she'd set in the drainer. "There is a dishwasher," he said, indicating the appliance beside the sink.

She shrugged. "There weren't that many, and I didn't have anything else to do."

They worked in silence for a few minutes, but with each second that passed, she was more aware of him beside her. The scent of him—not a cologne or aftershave, but the natural male essence of him; the heat emanating from his body, a body that had once merged with hers as if they were two halves of a whole, each incomplete without the other.

He'd once been everything to her, and when she'd lost him, she'd lost everything.

She rinsed the last dish, set it in the rack, then drained the soapy water.

"Coffee's ready," Nick said.

She hesitated to accept the implied invitation. The last thing she wanted was to spend any more time than was absolutely necessary in Nick's company. But after so many years of avoidance, maybe it was past time they did learn to coexist with one another again. Maybe she needed to face those memories to get past them.

So she nodded her head and said, "Coffee sounds good."

He grabbed two mugs from the cupboard, filled them both with the fresh brew, and passed one to her.

"Thanks." She moved to the refrigerator to get the cream, then carried it to the table. She added a generous splash to her cup along with a heaping teaspoon of sugar.

Nick took his own mug and pulled out the empty chair across from her. She noticed that he drank his coffee black.

She also noticed, as it was his left hand wrapped around the mug, that his wedding ring was gone. The last time she'd been home, he'd worn a simple gold band on his third finger and a gorgeous blonde on his arm. She wondered at the absence of both, and more so, why it mattered.

"How long were you planning on staying in Pinehurst?" Nick asked. "A couple of days? A week?"

"I don't know."

"Don't you have some hotshot job you need to get back to?"

She knew he was baiting her, but forced herself to respond coolly. "Yes, I have a job. But even hotshot attorneys are entitled to days off."

"I'm sure they are," he agreed. "Except that you don't strike me as the type of woman to take any."

And she never had before. In all the years she'd been at Dawson, Murray & Neale, she'd never taken a single personal day or sick day. Still, it rankled that he'd guessed this about her.

"What type of woman do I strike you as?" she challenged.

"Ambitious. Focused. Committed."

She could be all of those things—had been all of those

things. But lately she'd started to question her ambitions, lose her focus. And although nothing could have kept her away from Pinehurst after she'd learned of Caleb's accident, she couldn't deny that she was hoping a few days away from her job would give her a chance to reevaluate her choices, her life.

"Except that dropping everything to come back here seems both reckless and impulsive," Nick continued, then he smiled. "Which almost reminds me of the girl I used to know."

The smile was her first real glimpse of the Nick she remembered—the carefree boy who'd laughed easily and had made her laugh. If she'd been reckless and impulsive, it was because she'd been with him, because she'd trusted him implicitly and loved him completely.

"I'm not that girl anymore. I haven't been for a long time."

"I think you haven't let yourself be."

She shook her head, even though she knew there was some truth in what he'd said. She'd gone to great lengths to build an orderly and structured life for herself, because she was afraid of the impulses that had led her into his arms and terrified of the emptiness that had almost overwhelmed her when he'd gone. "You don't know anything about me or my life."

"I know that you can change your appearance but not your nature. I know that beneath the fancy suit and cool disdain, your blood still runs hot and your heart still beats faster when I'm with you."

She drained the last of her coffee, pushed her chair away from the table and stood up. "And I know that you've always been arrogant and delusional."

She started to turn away, but he grabbed her arm. She

felt a jolt of heat as his hand came into contact with her bare skin, and her heart leapt in response to the touch.

"I'm not imagining the way your pulse is racing right now," he said.

"Let go of me."

"That's a mistake I made once before."

She tugged her arm out of his grasp. "I didn't come here to play games with you, Nick."

"It doesn't matter why you came," he said. "It doesn't matter that I don't want you here. What matters is that there's still a powerful chemistry between us."

"Maybe it's just animosity," she shot back over her shoulder as she exited the room.

"There is that," he agreed.

Nick watched her walk away, wondering what it was about her cool, hands-off attitude that made him want to put his hands all over her. Maybe it was lust, a need to sate the physical urges that had been denied too long.

But as much as he wanted to believe it could be that simple, he knew it wasn't. Because he didn't just want the mindless physical release of sex. He wanted Jessica.

It had been eighteen years since they'd been together. Eighteen years after only one night, and yet he'd never forgotten anything about her. A fact that had been obvious to his wife—now his ex-wife—when Jess had returned to Pinehurst six years earlier.

"Tell me about her," Tina demanded.

Nick rubbed weary hands over his face. They'd just returned home from the cemetery after burying his mother and the last thing he wanted was to go another round with his obviously unhappy wife. "Who?"

Her eyes narrowed. "Jessica."

He shrugged, deliberately casual. "She's Kristin's best friend."

"I'm not interested in Kristin's relationship with her, I'm interested in your *relationship with her."*

"I've known Jess since she was seven years old." He hoped the information would placate her, stop her from digging at the scab over old wounds.

But Tina was nothing if not tenacious. "How long have you been in love with her, Nick?"

He'd denied her accusation vehemently. He'd even believed his denials. He never would have married Tina if he'd been in love with anyone else. Yes, he and Jess had a past—but it was in the past. Tina was his future.

For six months after that showdown, they'd continued to try to make their marriage work. In the end, Tina had walked out, and Nick had been relieved when she'd left. Although he'd refused to admit that he could still have feelings for Jessica, he'd realized that he hadn't loved his wife the way she'd needed to be loved.

The most bizarre part of their breakup was that, after the fact, Tina had encouraged him to go to New York, to find Jessica and resolve whatever was unresolved between them.

Nick had done so, just to prove her wrong. To prove that there wasn't anything unresolved between him and Jess— that they were simply former lovers who'd each gone their own way.

But when he'd tracked her down at Dawson, Murray & Neale, he'd found her in a conference with another lawyer. A man who looked as if he'd been born in his Armani suit—smooth, polished, professional. Nick hated him on sight. Even more so when Jessica introduced him as Steven Garrison—her husband.

He'd offered stilted congratulations to the happy couple, then excused himself on the pretext of having to get to a meeting, his reason for being in the city. He drove back to Pinehurst, convinced that the only thing left between him and Jess was history.

It was the last time he'd seen her.

Until today.

But now she was back, also divorced, and he was having a hard time remembering all the things that had gone wrong between them, all the reasons they were so obviously wrong for each other. Instead, all he could think about was how right everything had been when they were together.

He dumped the rest of his coffee down the drain, set his mug in the dishwasher, and headed out to his Explorer.

He'd promised to help Brian out with football practice this afternoon, hoping it would distract them both from their worries about Caleb. Nick hoped it would also make him forget about Jessica's return.

But as he headed toward the high school, he knew he was kidding himself. Nothing except Caleb's waking up would alleviate his concerns about his nephew. And as much as he enjoyed working with the team, he couldn't expect one afternoon on a football field to accomplish what eighteen years had failed to do—banish thoughts of Jessica Harding from his mind.

Chapter Three

Kristin stood in front of the window overlooking the hospital courtyard, staring down at the colorful and unoccupied playground equipment. She could all too easily picture Caleb climbing the rope ladder to the top of the slide or fearlessly hanging upside down on the monkey bars. It was what he should be doing—running and jumping and laughing.

Instead he was fighting for his life, and she didn't know how to help him. All she could do was wait.

It seemed as though she'd been waiting forever, even though she knew it couldn't have been more than twenty minutes since they'd taken Caleb away. Another CT scan, the orderly had explained, wheeling her child out of the room with brisk efficiency.

It seemed that everyone who worked here was brisk and efficient. The doctors, the nurses, even the janitorial staff. They moved through the narrow halls with an air of authority, a sense of purpose. While she hovered uncertainly on the periphery, waiting for someone, anyone, to tell her what the hell was going on.

And when she finally managed to catch someone's attention, the response would inevitably be a sympathetic smile, maybe a reassuring hand on her arm, and answers to her questions that somehow didn't give her any information at all.

Another X-ray.

But why?

What possible purpose would it serve?

How many times did they need to poke and prod at her baby before they finally figured out what was wrong?

Kristin wished she could have gone with him, just to hold his hand. She didn't want him to be afraid; she didn't want to admit that she was. Not just afraid, but terrified.

But she refused to give in to the fear. She had to stay strong, for Brian, for Jacob and Katie, and especially for Caleb. If there was any consolation at all, it was that her son had no idea what was happening. He couldn't see the needles and tubes and wires that made him look more like a dysfunctional robotic toy than the lively seven-year-old boy she knew him to be.

She glanced again at the clock on the wall, at the red hand that moved with agonizing slowness around its face. It was one of the strangest things about hospitals, she'd always thought, the way time seemed to stand still inside its walls while the world outside continued to function at a breakneck pace.

Twenty-one minutes.

And still she waited.

On the other side of the small room, Brian paced.

Restlessly, relentlessly.

Her husband had never been a patient person.

"I hate this," he said, his terse words punctuating the heavy silence like a bright flash of light through a thick fog. "The waiting."

Kristin nodded. She hated it, too, she was just more accustomed to it.

In fact, she'd practically made a career of waiting. She started her mornings early, then waited for the rest of her family to wake up so she could make their breakfast and see them off to work and school. Then she waited for the kids to come home again so she could take them to swimming lessons or basketball practice or art class. Everyone was in such a hurry these days—everyone but Kristin.

While Brian and Jacob and Katie and Caleb were rushing through their lives, Kristin was waiting.

And she hated it.

Finally the door swung open and Caleb's bed was steered back into the room.

She pushed off of the ledge, tentative flutters of hope stirring in her belly.

Please be awake. Please be awake. Please—

His eyes were still closed.

The flutters died, sinking like dead weight into the depths of her soul.

Kristin forced a smile for the benefit of a child who didn't even see her and lowered the rail on the side of the bed to take his hand. The one without the intravenous tube.

"Where's the doctor?" Brian demanded of the departing orderly.

"Doctor Marshall will be in to see you as soon as he's reviewed the test results," he said, then exited the room.

Brian resumed his pacing.

Kristin could understand his agitation. They were both upset, under a lot of strain.

She squeezed Caleb's hand gently, held her breath.

His fingers remained motionless.

She exhaled shakily, felt the sting of tears. Tears of anger and frustration. Tears of guilt.

She closed her eyes and leaned down to press a soft kiss to his pale cheek.

I'm so sorry, baby. So sorry.

But apologies were useless. Caleb needed more than her tears and regrets. He needed a miracle.

"I'm going to find the doctor before I head out to practice," Brian told her.

"Okay." There was no point in arguing. He would do what he needed to, and so would she.

But she hated being alone almost as much as she hated the waiting. Because when she was alone she couldn't block out the negative thoughts that went through her mind: what if the swelling in Caleb's brain didn't go down? What if he didn't come out of the coma? What if he suffered permanent brain damage? What if he—

No, she refused to even complete that thought.

Instead, she reached toward the pile of books that Katie had brought to the hospital. Katie, who at fifteen still thought of her little brother as a big pain in the butt, had sorted through all of Caleb's things, carefully selecting his favorite books and toys, to provide him with as many familiar things as possible in case—*when*—he woke up.

She picked up the first book and began to read.

Jessica paused outside of Caleb's hospital room, the top of the paper take-out bag crumpled in her fist, and listened to the soft, even rhythm of Kristin's voice. She hesitated, not wanting to interrupt if Caleb had other visitors, but as Kristin's monologue continued without interruption, she realized her friend wasn't talking, but reading. She couldn't hear the words, only the steady reassuring murmur of her voice.

Her heart broke for Kristin. When Jess had miscarried late in her second month of pregnancy, she'd been devastated. It was as though she'd lost a part of herself that could never be replaced, a vital piece without which she could never be complete. Even now, so many years later, she felt the pang of the loss, the emptiness that couldn't be filled.

She knew it would be a million times worse for a mother to lose a child with whom she'd already bonded. A child she'd carried inside her own body for nine months and birthed and nurtured at her breast. A child she'd soothed when he cut his first tooth, whose hand she'd held when he'd taken his first steps, a child for whom she'd cried tears of pride and joy and sadness when he'd gone off to his first day of kindergarten.

Jess knew Kristin had done all of these things because she'd told her about them in her letters. Jess had loved reading about each and every one of Kristin and Brian's children and had shared in the experiences vicariously.

Listening to her now, Jess imagined it was a favorite story she was reading. A book she'd enjoyed with each of her children through the years, the pages worn from countless turning, the pictures forever imprinted in their minds.

She heard a softly spoken, "The end," and a weary sigh before Kristin asked her son, "Shall we read it one more time, or have you had enough of the nut-brown hares?"

"I bet Caleb wouldn't mind if his mom took a break for dinner," Jess suggested, stepping into the room.

Kristin glanced up, surprise and gratitude evident in her tired eyes. "I didn't expect you'd be back tonight."

"I thought you might be hungry."

"Not really."

The response was what Jess had expected. "You should eat anyway."

Kristin sighed again. "I know. I just can't stomach the thought of food right now."

"It's pasta—from Mama Leone's."

"Caleb's favorite," her friend said softly.

"It used to be yours, too." She handed the bag to Kristin, then moved around to the other side of the bed and gently kissed Caleb's cheek. "We'll get you some Mama Leone's as soon as these tubes are gone," she promised him.

When she looked up again, she saw Kristin staring at her, her eyes filled with tears. "Thank you," she whispered.

"For the pasta?"

Kristin shook her head. "For not pretending he isn't here."

A single tear slipped onto her cheek and she turned away, busying herself with the unpacking of dinner. "There have been people in and out of here all day," she said. "Neighbors, friends from church, parents of Caleb's classmates. So many of them came to see me and Brian, to express their sympathy, offer their prayers. And so many of them refused to look at Caleb, as if his condition is contagious and tragedy might bleed into their perfect lives."

"I'm sure it's not intentional," she said gently.

"I know. I'm just pissed off at everyone right now."

"I'd guess that's normal."

Kristin laughed shortly. "Nothing about this is normal,

but we're doing the best we can under the circumstances." She began scooping angel-hair primavera onto two paper plates.

"Where's Brian?"

She thought she heard Kristin sigh. "He had to go to football practice."

"Oh." She accepted the plate and fork her friend passed to her.

"It's hard for him to be here," Kristin said, just a little defensively. "To see Caleb like this."

"I don't imagine it's easy for anyone," Jess said gently.

"No, but it helps Brian to go through the motions of a normal day."

She only nodded.

Kristin picked up a fork and twirled it in the pasta, set it down again without eating. "I thought the medication they're giving him would have taken effect," she admitted. "That he'd be awake by now."

"It's after eight o'clock," Jess said. "If he was awake, wouldn't you be telling him to close his eyes and get some sleep?"

Her friend managed a smile. "Yeah, I probably would." She toyed with a slice of red pepper. "Or maybe not. Right now I'd be so thrilled, I'd let him stay up until midnight if he wanted."

She closed her eyes for a moment, as if imagining the happy event. Then her eyes flew open. "I'm a horrible mother. I didn't even ask about Jake and Katie, if they had dinner."

"You're a wonderful mother," Jess said. "And they were ordering pizza when I left."

"I feel like I'm falling down on the job, but I can't seem to think about anyone but Caleb right now."

"They understand why you need to be here. And they seem pretty self-sufficient anyway."

"Yeah, they are that." There was pride, and a hint of sadness, in her voice.

"Since they obviously don't need a babysitter," Jess continued, "I was wondering if there was some other way I could help you out, something I could do for you."

"That isn't necessary."

"I want to help, Kristin."

"Why?"

"Because I hope being here now can somehow make up for neglecting our friendship for so many years."

Kristin was quiet for a moment. "I sometimes wondered if you were too busy to realize you were neglecting it."

"No," Jess admitted. "I knew."

Kristin nodded.

"I'm sorry—for so many things."

She set her plate aside. "Some of my earliest and happiest memories are of times we spent together. When you moved to New York, I didn't worry that we'd drift apart because I believed we were too close to ever let anything come between us.

"But eighteen years is a long time, and a handful of visits and occasional phone calls aren't enough to sustain the kind of connection we once shared."

"I know," Jess agreed.

"I missed you," Kristin said softly. "For a long time, I missed you. And then, somewhere along the line, I got used to you being gone."

She could only nod, her throat too tight to speak. It was her own fault, Jess knew that. She'd made the choice to decline Kristin's invitations to come home. She'd had her reasons, of course, but eighteen years ago those reasons had been too painful to share with anyone, even her best friend.

Now she thought she could probably talk about it and not fall to pieces. *Maybe.* But now wasn't about making excuses and explanations for what had happened so many years before. Now was about being here for Kristin, if she would let her.

"I really want to stay mad at you," Kristin said, "but I just don't have the energy right now."

It wasn't forgiveness, but it was a start.

"Do you really want to help?"

"Of course," Jess said quickly.

Her friend hesitated, as if reluctant to ask anything of her, as if she expected her to refuse.

"For the past few months I've been working in Nick's office, just a few hours a day, answering phones and filing orders."

Uh-oh. Like a runaway train, Jess could see where this was going but had no idea how to stop it. She could only brace herself and wait for the inevitable collision.

"Obviously I won't be able to be there for the next couple of days, and I hate to leave him in the lurch."

"I, uh, I really don't have any experience with that kind of work."

"Of course," Kristin said coolly. "You'd have a secretary of your own for such things."

Jess sighed. "That's not what I meant."

"What did you mean?"

"Just that Nick might prefer to hire someone from a temp agency—someone who would know what they were doing."

"He tried that when his secretary went off on maternity

leave, but the agency has a policy against sending staff to residential premises. That's why I've been helping him out."

"I don't know," Jess said uneasily.

"It's not rocket science, Jessica. I'm sure someone with two college degrees can figure it out."

It was a challenge, and probably the last opportunity Kristin would be willing to give her to make amends. As much as Jess wanted to limit her interactions with Nick, she couldn't refuse her friend's request.

"Then I'll try to figure it out."

It was almost nine-thirty when Jessica left the hospital. Despite the circumstances of her visit, she'd enjoyed sitting and talking with Kristin. Their conversation had been a little strained, but not nearly as uncomfortable as she'd expected given the tension she'd felt between them earlier that day. At least, not until Kristin had maneuvered Jess into helping out in Nick's office.

It wasn't that she had any objection to the type of work—it was the idea of being close to Nick that made her uneasy. In fact, everything about Nick made her uneasy. She didn't want to believe that she still had unresolved feelings for him—not after so many years had passed.

But even hours after their confrontation earlier that day, she was still unsettled. She decided to walk off her restless energy.

She set out without any particular destination in mind, yet when she found herself following the well-worn path through the trees at the back of Kristin and Brian's property, she'd known it was inevitable that she'd end up here. The pull of the memories was simply too strong to resist.

The wrought-iron bench on the bank of the creek had

been there for as long as she could remember. She ran a hand over the curved back, the metal cool and smooth beneath her palm. She lowered herself onto the seat, folded her knees against her chest, wrapped her arms around them. Then she tipped her head back to look at the sky and finally let herself remember.

She'd charmed an unopened bottle of champagne out of the bartender and slipped through the back of the tent into the darkness. It was only after she'd made her way down to the creek that Jess realized she'd forgotten a glass. She decided it didn't matter—she could just as easily drink a toast to her best friend without one.

It was harder than she'd anticipated to work the cork out of the bottle, but at last it gave way with a satisfying "pop." She heard a slight rustle of leaves as it sailed into the trees, and was grateful there had been no witnesses to her struggling ineptitude. There was no one around at all—the bride and groom had gone long ago, the rest of the guests shortly after.

But Jess wasn't ready to go home. Not yet.

She stood on the edge of the mossy bank, under the light of the moon and the stars, and took a sip of champagne directly from the bottle. The bubbles danced on her tongue, tickled her throat. She'd decided, after the single glass she'd had with dinner, that she quite liked champagne and didn't understand why it was typically reserved for special occasions.

She took another sip and tried to remember how many times she'd sat in this very spot with her best friend, sharing hopes and dreams for their future. But with Kristin and Brian's wedding, their lives had taken different directions, and the realization made Jessica's heart sigh. Even as she was looking forward to new opportunities, she couldn't help but mourn the childhood she was leaving behind.

She heard another rustling in the leaves, and her heart skipped a beat before it started pumping again, just a little stronger and faster than before. Because she knew, even before she turned to see him step through the trees, that it was Nick. Just as she knew that whatever her purported reasons for coming out here, she'd really been waiting for him.

"I thought everyone had gone," he said.

"Almost everyone."

He eyed the bottle in her hand. "Where'd you get that?"

"The bartender."

"You're underage, Jess."

"If my best friend's old enough to get married, surely I'm entitled to have a drink at her wedding."

"A drink, maybe," he agreed, deftly removing the bottle from her grasp. "Not a dozen."

She pouted. "Go away, Nick."

He studied her for a long moment, his gaze dark and inscrutable. "I should," he said at last.

"Then do it. You certainly didn't have any trouble ignoring me earlier tonight."

"What are you talking about?"

"I'm talking about the fact that you danced with almost every woman at the reception tonight—except me."

His gaze shifted guiltily. "I think that's a slight exaggeration."

She shook her head. She knew, because she hadn't been able to tear her eyes off of him all night, hadn't stopped hoping he would turn to her, take her in his arms. Just a dance— that was all she'd wanted. An innocent memory to lock away in her heart and take with her when she was gone.

But he'd denied her that. And now he was refusing to even acknowledge the slight.

"Every one except Barb Kenner, who was attached at the hip to her new fiancé, your Aunt Helen, who can barely walk because of her arthritis, and me."

"It wasn't a deliberate oversight."

"Wasn't it?"

He scrubbed a hand through his hair and sighed. "Hell, I don't know, Jess. Maybe it was."

She felt the sting of tears at the back of her eyes and cursed the fact that Nick had always been painfully honest with her.

"Do you want the truth?" he asked.

She swallowed, not sure if her bruised heart could survive another beating tonight. "Maybe not."

"Coward."

She lifted her chin so that she could glare at him.

He chuckled. "You're so predictable."

"And you're such an ass."

Nick took a step closer, traced a finger along the top of her dress, over the swell of her breasts. She sucked in a breath as her skin heated, burned, in response to his touch. The last traces of amusement in his eyes faded, gave way to something deeper. Something that both thrilled and terrified her.

"The truth is—" he dropped his hand away, took a careful step back "—from the moment I saw you standing at the back of the church in this dress, all I could think about was how much I wanted to get you out of it."

"How—" She needed to take a breath, because the way he was looking at her—as he'd never looked at her before—had sucked all of the air from her lungs. "That doesn't explain why you didn't want to dance with me."

"I didn't want to dance with anyone else," he said. "But I knew that if I touched you, if I held you in my arms, I wouldn't be able to let you go."

"Oh."

His lips curved into a wry smile. "Yeah."

She moistened her suddenly dry lips with the tip of her tongue, saw that the subconscious action had his gaze zeroing in on her mouth. Her heart hammered in her chest. "Dance with me now, Nick."

He shook his head. "Have you heard anything I've said?"

"Every word."

She breached the distance he'd deliberately put between them, flattened her hands against his chest. She could feel the beat of his heart, as strong and fast as her own, beneath her palms, and it emboldened her.

"Dance with me," she said again.

As if of their own volition, his arms came around her, drew her nearer. Even as her mind warned that she was playing a dangerous game, her body melted against his. She closed her eyes, her mind spinning, her heart singing, as she swayed in the darkness of the night with him to the music of gurgling water and chirping crickets.

His hands skimmed up her back, and down again. The slow seduction of his touch made her yearn, tremble. She shifted closer, and felt the press of something hard against her belly. This evidence of his arousal didn't surprise her as much as the answering, aching heat that pulsed deep inside her.

He dipped his head and pressed his lips to her throat. She sighed his name as the heat of desire escalated to burning need. His tongue stroked over her collarbone, fleeting, teasing caresses. Her hands gripped his shoulders tighter as the world seemed to tilt crazily beneath her.

Then, finally, he kissed her.

The brush of his mouth against hers was softly persuasive, but Jess didn't need any persuading. She'd wanted this, wanted him *for so long. She slid her arms around his neck, let her fingers sift through the silky hair at the nape of his neck. Her lips parted willingly when he deepened the kiss, her tongue eagerly meeting and mating with his.*

She didn't know how long the kiss lasted. Minutes? Hours? Days? There was no time or place, just an endless spiral of pleasure. And, when he finally drew back, an aching sense of disappointment that it hadn't lasted nearly long enough.

He exhaled an unsteady breath and leaned his forehead against hers. "You need to tell me to stop, Jessica."

"Why?"

"Because I don't have enough willpower to walk away on my own."

She loved him for wanting to make sure it was her choice. Then again, she'd always loved Nick. And loving him meant there was only one choice to make.

She met his gaze evenly, spoke clearly. "I don't want you to walk away."

He kissed her again, then lowered her onto the soft grass under the stars.

Chapter Four

"I wondered if you'd find your way out here while you were home."

Jessica glanced up to see Nick standing at the edge of the trees, the fringes of her dream. It was an oddly discomfiting sensation—this blurring of past and present. She blinked away the bittersweet reminiscence and accepted the harshness of reality.

"This is private property," she reminded him.

"Uh-huh." Despite his easy agreement, he came toward her.

"Which means you're trespassing."

He sat down beside her. "Actually *you* are."

Her brow furrowed. "I thought this was part of your parents' land."

"It was. After my mom died, we subdivided the property. The dividing line runs somewhere through the trees behind us."

"Who owns this part now?"

He smiled. "I do."

"Oh." She hugged her knees closer to her chest. "Do you want me to leave?"

"No." He paused a moment before saying, "I haven't been out here in years. And I didn't know what made me come out here tonight—until I saw you."

Uncertain how to respond to his revelation, she said nothing.

"What brought you out here, Jess?"

There were so many possible answers to that question. She decided the simplest was probably the best. "The stars."

"You don't have stars in New York City?"

"Not like this," she admitted. "It's like a completely different world here."

"A world you were anxious to leave behind."

She nodded. "I needed to be more than I could have been here."

He sighed. "You were the only one who could never see beyond the limits to the possibilities."

"In New York, there are no limits. Only endless possibilities."

"You're happy there?"

"I have a good life. A busy life." Which, they both knew, wasn't exactly an answer to his question. It was something she would think about later, when his presence wasn't wreaking havoc on her senses.

"No regrets?"

"I don't imagine anyone gets to this stage of life without a few."

"Probably not," he agreed.

She hesitated, then decided it was time to take that next step. "One of my biggest regrets is that I let what happened one night ruin a friendship we'd shared for so many years."

"You had to know things would change."

"I didn't expect they'd change so completely."

Nick didn't say anything.

She sat beside him in the silence until the shrill ring of her cell phone violated the quiet of the night. Jess unclipped it from her waist and glanced at the illuminated display. Recognizing the number, she wished she'd left the phone in the house. But she'd got in the habit of carrying it everywhere with her, to ensure she was never out of touch if anyone from the office needed to reach her. As was apparently the case now.

"I have to get this," she said to Nick.

He shrugged easily. "Go ahead."

She rose to her feet and took several steps away before flipping open the phone to connect the call. "Hello?"

"Where the hell are you, Jessica?"

She pushed her hair away from her face, ignored the automatic spurt of irritation that was just as likely to have stemmed from the identity of the caller as the tone of his question. "I'm in Pinehurst—as explained in my memo."

"Yes, your request for personal time—which wasn't approved before you took off," her ex-husband reminded her.

She lowered her voice, softly pleading for his understanding. She'd never asked him for any kind of favor, not even during their short-lived marriage, and she hoped he was cognizant of that fact now. "Please, Steve. I need to be here."

"For how long?"

"I don't know."

"You have responsibilities to this firm—including a meeting with Harrison Dekker scheduled for eight o'clock tomorrow morning."

Dekker Industries was one of the firm's largest clients and it had always irked Steve that the president of the company refused to work with anyone but her. "I already talked to Harrison—and Peter has agreed to cover the meeting for me."

"If those are the arrangements you've made, that's your choice. But you should know that with the partnership on the table, this isn't a good time to be away from the office."

It was a threat and not a particularly subtle one. Then again, subtlety had never been one of Steve's strengths. When they'd been dating, he'd let her know he was in the mood for sex by leaving a condom on the bedside table. His idea of a proposal had been for his secretary to check with her secretary to arrange a mutually convenient time for them to visit City Hall. And Jessica had been so pathetically grateful that she would no longer have to go home to an empty apartment, she'd pretended it didn't bother her.

"I'll keep that in mind," she said tersely, wondering why she'd ever expected that, even after years of dedication to the firm, he would show a little more understanding about a personal emergency.

She turned off the phone before tucking it away.

But not before Nick noted the faint furrow between her brows. "Problem?"

"Just my office," she said by way of explanation.

"I didn't realize that attorneys were so indispensable."

"I'm a hotshot attorney," she reminded him with a wry grin. "And I'm on the short list to make partner this year."

"Partner?" He made a show of sounding impressed. "Well, that really is a coup."

"I've worked my butt off for this opportunity."

"I'm sure you have," he agreed easily.

Her eyes narrowed. "What's that supposed to mean?"

"Just an acknowledgment that your career has always been your number one priority."

She didn't deny it.

"What was so important that your ex-husband had to track you down on a Sunday night?"

"He just wanted to know how long I expected to be out of the office, so that he could cover my schedule."

"How considerate of him."

"Yeah, Steve's a considerate guy."

Nick's lips twitched. "I might have believed that if I hadn't seen you roll your eyes."

"We frequently have differences of opinion," she admitted.

"Is that why you divorced?"

"Actually we used to get along fine—until I disagreed with his decision to sleep with his secretary."

"Ouch."

She nodded. "It hurt, not just the fact that he'd been screwing around, but that he'd done so with her. It's such a tired cliché."

He didn't know why she was telling him any of this, except that it was probably easier for her—as it was for him—to talk about a past that didn't involve the two of them. And it was infinitely easier to talk about the past rather than her reasons for being here in the present: Caleb's accident.

He stood up, took a step toward her. "I'm sorry, Jessica."

She shrugged. "Apparently I'm better with the law than relationships."

"What happened with the secretary?"

"He married her before the ink was even dry on our divorce. They have two kids now and two more on the way. Two sets of twins—she always was eerily efficient."

He smiled at the wry humor. "Did you love him?"

She opened her mouth to respond, closed it again, the furrow in her brow reappearing. "I thought I did," she said at last. "But now I think what we entered into was more of a merger than a marriage."

He knew it would be a mistake to touch her, but he reached for her anyway, cupping a hand under her chin, forcing her to meet his gaze. He saw the awareness in the widening of her eyes, heard it in the thunderous beating of his own heart. He inhaled the soft feminine scent she wore, felt the ricochet of the sparks zinging between them.

"The woman I once knew had too much passion to ever settle for anything less than everything."

She pushed his hand away. "The woman you knew was a girl—a teenager who didn't know how to control her runaway hormones."

"And your excuse for marrying a man you didn't love is that you no longer felt passion?"

"I grew up. I realized that there were more important considerations than desire."

"Other considerations—yes," he agreed. "More important—no way."

She shook her head, but he could tell she was fighting the smile that tugged at her lips. "Therein lies the basic difference between women and men."

He wanted to draw her nearer, to fold her into his arms,

feel the curves of her body yield against him. But he fisted his hands at his sides and held his ground. "Are you suggesting that you're no longer swayed by temptation?"

"I'm just saying that…um…sex…isn't the answer to every question."

He smiled, inordinately pleased by the realization that the usually unflappable Jessica Harding was obviously flapped by the topic. "Maybe not the whole answer," he agreed. "But it's a factor that shouldn't be ignored."

"Yes, well, as…um…interesting as this conversation is, I should be getting back to the house."

He considered asking her to stay. And maybe she would have. But he wasn't sure if either one of them was ready for any progress in their relationship beyond the fragile truce they seemed to have established.

"I'll walk with you," he said.

"I know the way."

He held his hand out to her. "I'll walk with you, anyway."

After a brief hesitation, she laid her palm against his. He closed his fingers around hers, disturbed by how natural it felt to be touching her, how comfortable he felt with her.

Even as she fell into step beside him, he cursed himself for being a fool. But he'd always been a fool where Jessica was concerned. He'd fallen in love with her when she was sixteen, proposed to her when she was seventeen. He'd been three years older, but still young enough and naive enough to believe they would be together forever.

He'd honestly thought they would build a life together—until she'd chosen her career over everything else.

Yeah, he might still want her, but he couldn't ever forgive her.

* * *

Jess stepped into the house, bolted the door behind her and exhaled a long, deep breath.

It had been close there for a second. For just the briefest moment as they'd stood together under the moon and the stars, she'd thought he was going to kiss her. For that brief moment, as the heady masculine scent of him tantalized her senses and her hands ached to slide over the firm muscles of his chest and shoulders, she'd wondered what would happen if he did kiss her. Would she push him away? Or pull him closer?

It had been a second of insanity. There and gone so quickly she wasn't sure if it had existed anywhere outside of her mind. Except that her heart was still beating a little too fast.

Which only proved to Jess how important it was to maintain a distance between herself and Nick, as she'd managed to do for the better part of eighteen years.

Unfortunately, circumstances were different now. If she and Nick both wanted to be available to Kristin and Brian, to support them, their paths would inevitably cross. Then there was the promise she'd made to Kristin to help out in Nick's office.

She sighed and rubbed a hand over her chest, trying to assuage the painful throbbing of her heart. It was ridiculous, really, to think that he could still have this effect on her after almost two decades. But maybe it wasn't Nick so much as the circumstances. It had been an emotional day all around, starting with the drive from Manhattan to her initial confrontation with Nick and seeing Caleb in the hospital. She was probably just worn out. She'd feel better in the morning, after a good night's sleep to recharge her batteries.

She removed the cushions from the sofa and pulled open the mattress. There weren't any sheets or blankets on the bed, so she tiptoed up the stairs in search of a linen closet, which she found, as expected, in the hall outside the main bathroom. She'd selected a set of sheets and was just closing the door when she heard the sound of muffled sobs. Pausing at the top of the stairs, she noticed a thin stream of light coming from another room further down the hall.

Katie's room.

She hesitated, reluctant to interfere but unable to ignore the girl's crying.

Jessica knocked softly on the partially opened door. "Katie?"

She heard a sniffle, something else that sounded distinctly like a nose being blown, then, "Yeah."

It wasn't exactly an invitation, but Jessica took it as such and stepped into the room.

She glanced around, noted the lavender color-washed walls, the white priscillas at the window, and the canopy bed. It was frilly and feminine, a perfect little girl's dream.

But the posters tacked up on every surface—rock groups and movie ads and teen heartthrobs—proved that Katie wasn't a little girl anymore. And then there was Katie herself, clad in her pyjamas—a pink camisole top and matching boxer shorts—sitting cross-legged on top of the covers, a math textbook open in front of her.

She and Jake both looked so much like Brian, with the same dark hair and dark eyes. But Katie also had her mom's delicate heart-shaped face, her sculpted cheekbones, and the same cupid's-bow mouth. She was a heartbreakingly beautiful girl, and Jess didn't doubt that her parents would have their hands full when she started dating.

It was almost enough to make her grateful she didn't have children of her own. *Almost.*

Now, however, with Kristin unavailable to respond to her daughter's needs, Jess figured it was her duty—and pleasure—as an honorary aunt, to fill in. But she also knew she'd have to tread carefully, not wanting to overstep her bounds with a girl who barely knew her.

Although it seemed like her own teenage years had passed a hundred years ago, she remembered the angst and anguish of high school, the worries about homework and boys and whether or not to go to the school dance or to the library to work on a science project. Okay, so it wasn't conflict in the Middle East, but to a fifteen-year-old, the consequences of a wrong decision could be just as disastrous. And with a brother fighting for his life in the hospital, Katie's worries were even greater than those of most girls her age.

Jess perched on the edge of the mattress. "You're worried about your brother, aren't you?"

Katie brushed her hands over her cheeks to erase the last traces of tears and nodded. "And Mom and Dad, and other stuff."

She frowned. "What about your mom and dad?"

"They're fighting again."

Jess swallowed the unease, suddenly feeling as though she'd landed herself in a minefield despite the careful treading. This wasn't at all what she'd expected. But now that the girl had confided in her, she couldn't ignore her concern. Although she was sure it wasn't anything to be concerned about—Kristin and Brian were as connected as any two people could be and still retain separate identities. "It's normal for married people to disagree," she said gently.

Katie looked at her, her dark eyes filled with tears that expressed a sadness and knowledge far beyond her years. "Are you married?"

It was more of a challenge than a question. "No," she admitted.

"Then how do you know?" Katie demanded.

"I was married," she said, then realized that the failure of that marriage wasn't likely to reassure the girl.

"What happened?"

She didn't see the point in revealing the details of her husband's infidelity, so all she said was, "We never fought."

Katie frowned.

Jess smiled. "It's true. I didn't see it as a problem at the time. I just thought we were so perfectly attuned to one another, there was no reason to argue or disagree. The truth was, we never talked about anything but work. We didn't know how to communicate."

"I don't see how fighting is a means of communication."

An astute observation for a fifteen-year-old, Jess thought. "It's an outlet for emotion," she explained. "And it's a difficult time for both of them—for all of you—right now."

The girl shook her head. "The arguing started way before Caleb's accident."

"I still don't think it's something you should be worrying about," she said. "And I'm sure your parents wouldn't want you to be worrying about it. Whatever difficulties they're having, it's up to them to work through them."

"I don't think they will," Katie said, her voice little more than a whisper. "Not this time."

Not this time. The words echoed in Jess's heart, filled her with a sense of foreboding. For eighteen years, she'd believed Kristin and Brian were happy. She'd *wanted* them to be happy. Because it was easier for her to cope with her own loneliness, to accept having sacrificed her friendship with Kristin knowing that she was so blissfully in love with her husband she wouldn't miss her best friend.

"You can't make their problems your own," she said gently.

"I know." But Katie didn't look convinced.

Jess tapped the textbook on the bed in an effort to draw the girl's attention away from her other concerns. "Having trouble with your homework?"

"A little," she admitted.

"What is it?"

"Algebra. Factoring trinomials."

"Really?" She breathed a sigh of relief. Finally a problem she could handle. "Want some help?"

"You can do this stuff?"

She laughed at the blatant skepticism in the question. "Believe it or not, yes, I can."

"Mom's not very good at math," Katie said, then ducked her head again, almost guiltily.

"She never was," Jess agreed. "But she's musically talented and she always excelled in geography."

"I didn't know that."

"Sure. I used to do—um, help her…with her math homework and she'd…help me with geography." She smiled at the memory. "No one could help me in music— I was hopeless."

"You were friends for a long time, weren't you?"

She wondered if her use of the past tense was intentional. "Since second grade."

"Caleb's in second grade this year."

They both fell silent.

"Why don't you bring that book downstairs?" Jess suggested. "I'll make us some hot chocolate and we can figure out trinomials together."

Katie offered a watery smile. "Okay."

Brian hated hospitals.

He'd been eighteen years old when he'd been taken down in an illegal tackle that had wrecked his shoulder and ended his professional football prospects. He'd been a shining star abruptly extinguished, with no hope for his future and only an unending series of surgeries ahead of him.

He'd been sent from one hospital to the next, but they were all the same. The overly bright fluorescent lights in endlessly long corridors. The incessant din of beeping machines and murmuring voices. And the pungent antiseptic smell that failed to cover up the lingering scent of sickness and death.

Mostly he hated the feeling of helplessness, the knowledge that everything was out of his control. He'd hated that feeling all those years ago, he hated it even more now.

Yeah, it had seemed like the end of the world when he'd found out his football career was over. But he'd got through that disappointment with Kristin by his side. He didn't know how either of them would get through this if Caleb didn't survive.

He'd been making excuses to get away from the hospital. He needed a distraction, but nothing could make him forget what had happened to Caleb. Kristin, of course, hadn't left their son's side for more than a few minutes at a time since he'd been brought in. While Brian appreciated her vigil, he couldn't participate in it.

Even now, he hesitated, unable to cross over the threshold into his son's room. He didn't want to see him like this; he didn't want to admit that any of this was real.

He could see his wife sitting on the edge of the bed. Still holding on to Caleb's hand, murmuring softly to him, as if she could will him back to consciousness.

And maybe she could. He'd never known anyone with the strength of will to match hers. During his numerous periods of hospitalization, he always remembered waking up to find Kristin holding his hand. Her support had been steadfast, her conviction absolute, her love an anchor in his sea of misery.

But a lot had changed in eighteen years.

Her blue eyes didn't sparkle anymore; her soft lips didn't curve anymore. She wasn't just grieving, she was empty. A shell of the beautiful, vibrant girl he'd once known.

And the changes had happened long before Caleb's accident.

He didn't know when it had all gone so wrong between them, only that it had. He didn't know if there was any way they could ever make things right again, only that he wished they could.

"Are you coming in?"

She asked the question without turning around, somehow sensing his presence.

Brian hesitated another second before stepping into the room. "Has Dr. Marshall been here tonight?"

Kristin shook her head.

He moved to the other side of the bed, took the chair facing Kristin. He didn't look at Caleb—he couldn't.

"Why don't you talk to him?" she suggested gently.

He wanted to, but his throat was tight. He only shook his head.

"Or touch him? Let him know you're here."

"I'm—I'm afraid I'll hurt him."

Her eyes were filled with sadness. "It would hurt him more to know that you can't even look at him."

She always could see right through him.

"Does that make me a horrible father—because I can't stand to see my son lying there? Because I can't stand to consider the possibility that he might never wake up?"

"No," she said softly, and reached across the bed to take his hand. "It just makes you a father."

Her understanding, her compassion, touched him and shamed him at the same time. She was giving him a chance to be the man she wanted him to be, but he couldn't be anything more than who he was.

"He needs you, Bri. He needs to know that we're both here for him."

"You mean like I wasn't there when all this happened?"

She pulled her hand away, her already pale cheeks turning pasty white. "No, that's not what I meant at all."

He could tell by the earnestness of her response that she was telling the truth. Or believed she was, anyway.

"Maybe it's just me," he admitted. "I can't help thinking that this might not have happened if I'd been there."

She blinked, looked away. "I was there," she reminded him softly. "And it happened anyway."

And he realized then that she didn't blame him—she blamed herself.

He could see the shimmer of tears in her deep blue eyes, trembling on the edge of her lashes. But she held them back, a hint of her youthful determination shining through.

This brief glimpse of the girl she used to be transported him back twenty years, to a time when their dreams had been both simple and innocent. A time when she'd been so beautiful, so vibrant and so full of life, and he'd been so much in love with her.

He looked at her now—at the woman who bore only a surface resemblance to that carefree girl.

He wanted to move closer, to put his arms around her, to pull her head down to his shoulder. But there'd been so much distance between them lately, so much uncertainty. He wanted to offer comfort, but he didn't know how—and he didn't know if she'd turn to him...or turn away.

It was the not knowing that held him back. Instead of reaching out to her, he looked away.

He pretended he didn't see her crying, and she pretended she wasn't.

Chapter Five

Jessica pushed herself up in bed and squinted at the clock on the desk. The glowing red numbers remained indecipherable.

She felt around on the floor beside the bed for her glasses, settled them on her nose. A few years ago, she'd needed only minimal vision correction. Now she couldn't find her glasses without her glasses on. Damn, but she hated getting older.

She looked at the clock: 7:27 a.m.

So much for getting the kids up—she couldn't even get herself out of bed.

She'd turned in around midnight but hadn't slept well. Long after she'd said good-night to Katie, she'd lain awake wrestling with her doubts and concerns about having come back to Pinehurst. But she didn't have time for doubts this morning.

She threw her legs over the side of the mattress, banging her calf on the metal frame. She rubbed the tender spot with one hand and reached for her robe with the other.

If the sounds coming from the kitchen were any indication, Jake and Katie were already up. Obviously they were more responsible than she was.

Coffee. She definitely needed coffee this morning—preferably a whole pot of it. She shoved her arms into the sleeves of her robe, made a quick stop at the bathroom to brush her teeth, then headed for the kitchen in search of a much-needed caffeine fix.

Jake was at the table, eating cornflakes out of what looked like a serving bowl. Katie was at the other side of the table, nibbling on a slice of unbuttered toast. They were both dressed, their backpacks sitting at the ready by the door. Neither seemed to take note of her presence.

Obviously they didn't need any help getting ready for school. And a good thing, too.

"Coffee?"

She yelped.

"Dammit, Nick. Why do you keep sneaking up on me?"

He grinned. "I didn't sneak. I was standing here when you came in."

"But what are you doing here?"

"Kristin asked me to stop by and pick up a change of clothes for her."

She frowned. "When did you talk to Kristin?"

"At the hospital this morning." Then, anticipating her next question, he gave a quick shake of his head. "No change."

Jessica felt a pang of disappointment as she reached into the cupboard for a mug. She thought of her friend, of the nighttime vigil she'd kept at Caleb's bedside, waiting, hoping, praying.

Jake pushed away from the table, then dumped his empty bowl and spoon into the sink.

"C'mon, Kate," Nick prompted. "You're going to be late."

She pushed away her half-eaten piece of toast and took a last sip of juice.

Jake hefted his backpack over his shoulder. "See you later, Uncle Nick. Jessica."

Katie scooped up her bag and followed her brother out the door, tossing a quick "bye" and a wave over her shoulder.

"She's not much of a morning person, is she?"

Nick just shrugged.

"Kristin never was, either," Jessica recalled, smiling at the memory of late-night slumber parties and early mornings after.

"She still isn't."

"How was she this morning?"

"As good as can be expected."

Jessica sipped her coffee.

"How are you this morning?" Nick asked.

The question, simple without any apparent trace of hostility or bitterness, surprised her. She eyed him warily. "Okay," she said hesitantly.

He laughed. "It wasn't a trick question."

"No, but it was almost…convivial."

"Convivial—that sounds like one of those overpriced lawyerly words."

She smiled. "Yeah—subtle digs and insults. That's more like the Nick I remember."

He grinned. "Sorry. I actually came over here this morning to apologize."

"For what?" she asked.

"For being pushy last night."

"You've always been pushy."

He grinned. "You've always known how to push back."

Her lips curved, just a little. "It was the only way to en-sure you couldn't steamroll me."

"Truce?"

She sighed. "Do you think it's that easy?"

"Probably not," he admitted. "But since circumstances keep throwing us together, I'm willing to try."

"Kristin told you about wanting me to help out in your office," she guessed.

He nodded.

"Did you nix the idea?" she asked hopefully.

"Should I have?"

She couldn't believe he had to ask that question. "I can't imagine you want me underfoot for several hours ev-ery day."

"It wouldn't have been my first choice, but I really do need the help." He lifted an eyebrow. "You're not trying to renege on your promise to Kristin, are you?"

"Of course not," she hedged. "I just want to make sure I'm available if she needs me for anything."

"If she does, she has the number for my office."

She nodded, reminding herself it was only for a couple hours a day. If he could handle it, so could she.

"Does that mean we have a deal?" He offered his hand.

After only the briefest hesitation, she placed her hand in his, felt the familiar frisson of heat as his fingers closed around hers. The hint of humor in his eyes faded to some-thing dangerous as tension shimmered around them.

"It seems unlikely, doesn't it, that something as simple as physical attraction could endure for more than eighteen years?"

She carefully withdrew her hand. "Unlikely," she agreed, trying to match his casual tone.

"Which makes me think that maybe it was never that simple."

It never had been. Not for Jess. She'd loved Nick with all her heart, until he'd shattered it into a billion sharp, jagged pieces.

"Right now we're both focused on Caleb," he continued. "As we should be. I'm just giving you fair warning that before you leave, we're going to have to deal with what's between us."

The dark promise in his eyes made her heart stutter, but she forced herself to respond lightly. "You always were a good sport, Nick."

His smile was thin. "I threw in the towel once. This time we'll see it through to the end."

"Don't I have any say in this?" She was trying for annoyance, was all too aware that her response came out sounding just a little breathless.

"I'm not sure either one of us does."

His gaze dipped to her mouth, lingered.

That was all—just a glance—and her lips were tingling with memories.

"I, uh, have to get to the hospital."

His smile was slow, easy. "I'll see you at the office at ten."

Jess could feel the tension in the room. It was obvious in the physical distance between Kristin and Brian and the abrupt tone of their conversation. She hovered in the doorway, uncertain whether to advance or retreat.

"Forget it," Brian said. "I have to go, anyway."

"You just got here."

Kristin's response didn't sound like a protest so much as an accusation.

"I have a lot of planning to do before practice this afternoon."

"Oh. Of course."

His sigh was filled with frustration. "Don't do this, Kristin. Not now."

"I'm not doing anything."

"Dammit, you're trying to make me feel guilty—"

"I'm not trying to make you feel anything," she denied.

Jess balanced the tray of coffee cups in one hand and knocked, loudly, with the other.

"Coffee's here." She smiled, overly brightly, as she stepped into the room.

Brian's answering smile was forced. "I'll have to take mine to go."

He bent to kiss his wife; Kristin turned so that his lips grazed her cheek.

Jess looked away, feeling embarrassed at having witnessed their strained interaction.

Without another word, Brian walked out the door.

They're fighting again.

Katie's words echoed in her mind.

She was right, Jess realized. She'd thought it possible that the girl had misinterpreted something or overreacted, but the brief exchange she'd overheard convinced her otherwise.

Jess handed another cup to Kristin, then pried the lid off of her own.

Kristin cradled the paper cup between her palms but made no attempt to drink from it. "You heard Brian and me arguing," she guessed.

She couldn't deny it, so she only shrugged. "It's a difficult time, for both of you."

"Yeah." Her friend sighed, as if there was more she wanted to say. But then she clammed up again.

The arguing started way before Caleb's accident.

How much before? Jess wondered.

Had Kristin and Brian been having difficulties for a long time? And who had Kristin turned to, to share her feelings and concerns? Who had been her friend when she wasn't around?

"If there's anything you want to talk about, I'd like to listen," Jess said softly.

Kristin seemed to consider the offer for a moment, then shook her head. "You've always been good at listening, Jess."

She frowned, wondering why her friend sounded so bitter about the fact.

"I was always the one who talked," she continued. "Even after you were gone—I talked to you through my letters."

Jess didn't know what she was supposed to say. "I always enjoyed your letters," she ventured. "When I read them, it was almost as if you were there, talking to me."

Kristin stared at the lid of her coffee cup. "You never wrote back."

She swallowed. "I did—"

"Okay, *never* was a slight exaggeration. How many letters did you send—maybe one or two a year? Not counting the annual Christmas card, of course, which shouldn't count anyway, since it was professionally engraved."

The anger and bitterness in the response shocked Jess. She'd never realized how much her silence had upset Kristin, how much she'd inadvertently hurt her friend.

"I wrote to you all the time," she admitted. "I just didn't send the letters."

Her confession silenced Kristin for a moment. Then she asked, softly, "Why?"

She sighed. "Because I had nothing to say."

"Nothing?"

Now it was Jessica who hesitated. "Nothing that seemed worthwhile.

"Dear Kristin, I went to class today and have another criminal law paper due next week.

"Dear Kristin, I got a part-time job tending bar at a pub near the law school.

"Dear Kristin, I went grocery shopping and found a sale on canned tuna.

"That was my life—uneventful, uninspiring. You have no idea how many letters I started to write, only to throw them away."

"I wished you'd sent them," Kristin said. "It wouldn't have mattered what was inside—only that they were from you."

"Writing those letters forced me to examine my life, and to realize how empty it was. By not sending them, I was at least able to maintain the illusion that my life was too busy and full to afford me time to write.

"I'd gone after what I wanted," she admitted, "but I envied what you had."

"Why didn't you ever tell me?"

"Because I felt like an idiot for being jealous of my best friend because I'd made different choices for my life." She forced a smile. "I found out a couple of months ago that I'm probably going to make partner this year."

"You don't sound very excited about it."

"I've worked my butt off for this for more than a dozen

years. It was my ultimate goal from the first day I started at Dawson, Murray & Neale.

"And yet, when I got the news, I actually had a moment of panic, thinking: is this really what I want for the rest of my life—to spend it working at a job that's sucking the life out of me?

"And then I sat down and really thought about it, and I realized that, without my job, I have nothing."

"What about your friends?"

Jess smiled. "You're my best friend, and look at the mess I made of that."

"I'd say we both messed up," Kristin said. "But that doesn't mean we can't fix it."

"I want to fix it," she admitted. "I want you to be part of my life again."

"Me, too." Kristin looked at her watch and smiled for the first time all morning. "But right now, you've got to get to work."

Jess stared at the neat, glossy black lettering on the textured cream background of the business card in her hand.

Armstrong & Sullivan Architects, Inc.
Custom Homes & Renovations

She compared the address to the number on the mailbox and pulled into the driveway.

Kristin had mentioned that Nick's office was in his home, but that information hadn't prepared her for the house. She sat in her car for a long moment and stared at the residence.

Although she knew next to nothing about architecture, she could still appreciate the beauty of the design. Two stories of warm red brick and gleaming multipaned windows set off by glossy black shutters.

She parked beside his vehicle. At least, she assumed the dark blue Explorer was his. But maybe it belonged to his partner—Sullivan. That possibility reassured her some- what. It would be easier to get through this with someone else around to act as a buffer between her and Nick.

Still, her trepidation increased with every step she took on the interlocking brick path that led to the door, where a discreet brass plaque confirmed she was at the right place. She took a deep breath and turned the knob.

Nick was in the outer office, his hip propped against the edge of the desk as he flipped through a sheaf of papers in his hand. He glanced up as she walked in, then his gaze flickered to the clock on the wall. "You're late."

"I got caught in traffic."

To her surprise, he grinned. "Had to stop for a red light?"

"Two of them." She dropped her purse on the desk, set- tled into the chair. "Is your partner in?"

"Mason prefers to work at his own place, but he usual- ly drops in once or twice a week, so I'm sure you'll get to meet him."

"Oh." So much for the buffer.

But Nick didn't seem concerned about a buffer or lack thereof. In fact, there was no hint of any of the sexual ten- sion she'd felt between them earlier as he set about explain- ing her duties in an efficient and completely professional manner. .

Even so, Jessica felt as though she was dancing around a live wire. When he reached over her shoulder to slide the mouse and click open the e-mail program, she could feel the heat emanating from his body and caught a whiff of his scent—clean and masculine. She could hear him talking, but nothing registered except his nearness. The close proximity was torture on hormones too long dormant. Or maybe the state of her hormones had nothing to do with dormancy and everything to do with Nick.

"Any questions?"

Her mind had been so busy wandering down a different path, she honestly couldn't remember anything he'd said to her in the past several minutes. She could only hope that Kristin was right—that someone with a college education could figure it out.

"Uh, no," she said.

He nodded, the glint of amusement in his eyes suggesting he might be aware of her mental detour. "I'll be in my office—if you want me."

Did she want him? What a question. But she had no intention of giving in to the traitorous desires.

Still, it wasn't until she heard his door close that she finally exhaled the breath she hadn't even realized she'd been holding.

Then the phone started ringing and she got busy answering calls and sorting through e-mails and Internet orders. She'd thought architecture was just about drawing pictures. She'd had no idea how technical or detailed those drawings were or that Nick also worked closely with his clients and engineers and contractors until a project was finished. The work gave her an insight into his career, a growing respect for the work he did, the business he'd built and the man he'd become.

It was after two o'clock when Nick finally emerged from the confines of his office. Although he usually wandered in and out of the reception area while Kristin was there, to stretch his legs or just chat with his sister, he'd decided it was wise to keep a closed door between him and Jessica at all times.

Knowing how wary she'd been about this temporary working arrangement from the outset, he'd have expected her to be out the door at precisely one o'clock. He was more than a little surprised to step out of his office and find she was still seated at the front desk, an array of folders spread out in front of her and a stack of documents in her hand that she was sorting through.

He'd tried to keep things distant, professional, when she'd arrived at his office earlier. Partly because he really needed her help and didn't want to tick her off enough that she'd walk out despite her promise to Kristin, and partly for purposes of self-preservation because—whether he wanted to accept it or not—she was getting to him. He was starting to forget his distrust and anger and remember how much he'd once enjoyed being with her.

He couldn't deny that he was drawn to her, but he knew that, like a moth to a flame, getting close to Jessica would inevitably result in his ending up burned. He wasn't going to let it happen again.

But that didn't mean he couldn't enjoy looking at her. That he couldn't admire the way the silky fabric of her blouse draped over the gentle swell of her breasts, or how the slim-fitting skirt hugged the dip of her waist and flare of her hips before ending just above her knees. At least, it was just above her knees while she'd been standing. But now that she was seated with her legs crossed, the skirt had shifted, exposing a few tantalizing inches of her thigh.

His gaze trailed from the hem of her skirt, over the

curve of her knee, down the shapely length of her calf to the narrow ankle and the slender foot tucked into low heels.

He'd always thought she had great legs. Long limbs, sleek muscles, creamy skin. And he remembered those long limbs wrapped around him—

He ruthlessly banished the memory.

She paused in her sorting, staring at one of the pages.

"Estimate or future project?" She mumbled the question to herself.

He took another step into the room, saw that her brow was furrowed. Glancing over her shoulder, he recognized the document she was scowling at as a faxed acceptance of a proposal.

"Future project," he said.

She nodded. "Which means I have to make a new file with the client's name."

"Actually, Jerry Leonard is a regular client so we'll already have a folder. Bottom drawer of the right-hand cabinet."

"Oh." She pushed the chair away from the desk and stood up, straightening her skirt as she did so.

No doubt about it—she still had great legs. His gaze followed her as she moved to the filing cabinet, crouched in front of the bottom drawer. His mouth watered.

He cleared his throat. "Didn't I explain this to you this morning?"

"Probably." She pulled open the drawer, found the file he'd indicated and slid the page inside. "After a few hours here, I have to admit that I have a whole new respect for my secretary."

"If you're finding it that torturous, why are you still here? Kristin would have bailed on me more than an hour ago."

"I didn't want to just walk out," she said. "I tried buzzing you a couple of times but your line was busy and I didn't want to interrupt."

She closed the drawer again and stood up, just as the front door opened and Mason Sullivan walked in.

"Nick, I've got—" He stopped abruptly, surprise—then pleasure—lighting his face when he saw Jessica. A smile creased his face. "Hel-lo."

Nick had known his business partner since college. He was easygoing, personable and charming, definite assets when it came to drumming up clients for the business. He also had a reputation as a heartbreaker—and Nick didn't like the way he was looking at Jessica.

"Are you looking for someone to build your dream home?" Mason asked her.

Jess smiled. "No."

"Someone to share your dream home?"

She chuckled. "No."

"Already married?"

"Not anymore."

"Then this must be my lucky day." He offered his hand and another smile. "Mason Sullivan."

She shook his hand. "Jessica Harding."

Nick's irritation continued to mount as he listened to the lighthearted banter between them. "Is there a reason you stopped by, Mason, other than to hit on my new secretary?"

He used the title deliberately, knowing it would irk Jess. The cool glance she sent over her shoulder told him he'd succeeded.

"You work for this guy?" Mason asked, still holding on to her hand.

"Only temporarily," she assured him.

"Maybe when you're finished here, you could come work for me."

She shook her head, finally extracting her hand from his grasp.

"Jess is a corporate attorney," Nick cut in. "She's only going to be in town for a short while."

"I could relocate," Mason said. "Where are you from, Jessica?"

"New York."

"Ah. The big city, full of bright lights and beautiful women."

"And this particular woman was on her way out," Nick said pointedly.

"I was," she agreed. "I want to see how Kristin's doing, then try to get something together for dinner for the kids."

"You can cook?" Mason asked.

"When I have to."

"Just so you know," Nick interrupted again, "Katie doesn't eat red meat and Jake doesn't eat scalloped potatoes, corn, beans or mushrooms."

"Oh. Okay."

He smiled. "But I'll eat anything if someone else is cooking it for me."

She picked up her purse off the corner of the desk. "Are you angling for an invitation to dinner?"

"I seem to have worked through lunch."

"You want a home-cooked meal, get a wife," she told him.

Mason hooted with laughter.

"I had one," Nick told her. "She never cooked for me, either."

"Maybe because it's hard to prepare anything resembling a main course in an Easy-Bake oven," Mason said dryly.

He sent a warning look toward his friend. "She wasn't *that* young."

"She was starting high school when you were graduating college."

"Okay, she was young," he agreed.

"As insightful as this conversation is," Jess interrupted, "I really do need to be going."

"What about dinner?" Nick asked.

She shrugged. "Fine. I'll try to have something ready for six o'clock."

"Do you want me to bring anything?"

"You can pick up dessert." Her lips curved. "Maybe a cake."

Mason laughed again. Nick glared at him, then followed Jessica to the door.

"Jess."

She paused with her hand on the doorknob.

"Thanks for filling in today."

"It wasn't a problem."

He smiled. "Yeah, it was. I know you didn't want to be here, and I appreciate the effort."

She smiled back. "Let's see if you're still grateful when you can't find anything I've filed." Then she turned to Mason. "It was nice meeting you."

"My pleasure."

Mason sighed wistfully when the door closed behind her. "Damn, she's hot."

If it had been any other woman he was talking about, Nick probably would have agreed, maybe even added some commentary of his own. But this was Jessica, and he didn't appreciate Mason panting over her—even if he'd been doing the same thing himself a few short minutes ago.

"What happened to Cassandra?" he asked, referring to his friend's latest girlfriend.

"She started making noises about marriage and babies." Mason shuddered.

Nick's tension eased and he laughed despite his annoyance. His partner was nothing if not predictable.

"Do you think Jessica would be interested in a commitment phobe like me?"

He shook his head. "Stay away from her."

Mason lifted an eyebrow. "Are you warning me because you're feeling protective—or proprietary?"

"She's a friend of my sister's," he said, aware that his response didn't really answer the question.

"Uh-huh." Mason's tone indicated that he understood what Nick hadn't said as much as what he had.

"Are those the blueprints for the Stilwells?" Nick asked, determined to change the topic.

"Yeah." His partner switched gears to keep up with him. "Nadine called this morning with 'just a couple more little changes.'"

"How little?" Nick asked warily.

Mason uncapped one of the cylinders. "Let me show you."

Nick bent his head over the papers Mason had spread out, but his mind was still with Jessica, and he was already looking forward to dinner when he would see her again.

Chapter Six

When Jess finally got back to Kristin and Brian's after a brief stop at the hospital and then the grocery store, Jake and a friend were playing one-on-one in the driveway. She parked at the curb so as not to interfere with their game and was gathering bags from the trunk when she heard Jake's sharp, "Heads up!"

She glanced up just in time to catch the basketball in her free hand.

"Sorry, Aunt Jess."

"No problem." She tossed it toward the hoop, smiling with satisfaction when it swished silently through the net.

"Wow." Jake's friend gaped at her.

Jake grinned. "Ethan, this is my Aunt Jess. She went to college on a basketball scholarship," he explained to his friend. Then to Jess he said, "This is Ethan. He's here to beg for dinner tonight."

"Seems to be a theme today," Jess said, pushing the trunk closed with her elbow.

"My mom works shifts," Ethan told her, dribbling the ball from one hand to the other. "When she's on afternoons, Mrs. Clarke usually lets me eat here. But I can find something at home if it's a problem."

"It's not a problem," she assured him. "So long as you're not a picky eater."

"He'll eat *anything,*" Jake said, stealing the ball and jumping to take a shot.

Ethan shrugged. "Can I give you a hand with those bags?"

"Thanks, but I think I've got it."

But he beat her to the back door, opened it for her. "How about shooting some hoops with us after you get that stuff inside?"

She was flattered by the offer. "I'm already behind schedule with dinner."

"Maybe later?" he asked.

She smiled. "Maybe."

Jess considered the invitation as she started to get dinner ready. Basketball had been her road out of this town, the ticket to her education. And yet, she hadn't played in years. She hadn't even thought about it in years. But she found herself thinking about it now, oddly tempted by the thought of playing again.

She'd set the chicken in the oven to bake, the potatoes on the stove to boil, and was just dumping a package of salad mix into a bowl when Nick came in.

He let himself in through the back door, obviously as comfortable in his sister's home as his own. Of course, his sister's home had once been his own, as they'd both grown up here.

"I brought dessert," he said, setting a square bakery box on the counter.

She found a cutting board and started to slice the cucumber. "Cake?" she couldn't resist asking.

"As a matter of fact, yes." He helped himself to a beer from the fridge, twisted off the cap. "Despite the jokes that you and Mason were cracking at my expense."

"I didn't say anything," she denied. "Except to make a suggestion."

"Did you suggest Black Forest cake?"

She wondered if he'd remembered or if it was merely a coincidence that he'd chosen her favorite. "No, but I must applaud your choice."

"Hmm." He took another swallow of beer. "That's almost exactly what Mason said. Of course, he wasn't talking about the cake, but you."

"Really?"

"My partner seemed quite impressed by you."

"Your partner seems like the type who would be impressed by anyone with a double-x chromosome."

Nick leaned back against the counter, grinned. "I don't think it was your…chromosomes that impressed him. But yeah, that's Mason. Although beneath the lady-killer exterior, he really is a nice guy."

"I'll take your word for it." She shut off the buzzer and pulled the chicken out of the oven.

"I heard you impressed someone else today, too."

She turned the breasts, sprinkled on some more spices, then returned the pan to the oven. "Who?"

"Ethan."

She smiled as she dumped the cucumber on top of the lettuce. "If I did, Ethan's easily impressed."

"Last season, Ethan averaged twenty-two points a game for the Senior Panthers. I don't think he's easily impressed."

"It was a free throw."

"From the bottom of the driveway."

"Yeah." She smiled again. "I guess it was a pretty good shot."

He snagged a slice of cucumber from the tossed salad. "You play much basketball in New York?"

She laughed. "Not in the past dozen years."

"Why not?"

She grabbed a tomato and started to cut it into wedges. "Lack of time and opportunity."

"I would have thought, if it was something you really wanted to do, you would have made the time."

"It's hard to make time when there are only twenty-four hours in the day and I'm at the office most of those."

"You're kidding."

She shook her head. "I usually work twelve hours a day, sometimes longer if there's a dinner meeting or business reception with clients. That doesn't leave much time to play basketball."

"Or anything else," Nick said.

"Or anything else," she agreed. "I don't even have houseplants because I was forever forgetting to water them and then feeling guilty when I finally realized they were dead and had to throw them out."

"What about a social life?"

She laughed. "My social life is nonexistent. I haven't had a date in more than six months and it's been at least twice that amount of time since I've had se—"

She stopped slicing and dropped her head forward. "Please tell me that I didn't actually say that last part out loud."

"The part about no sex in twelve months?"

She didn't need to look at him to know he was grinning. She groaned and closed her eyes. "I didn't say that."

"Not in so many words," he agreed.

"I really don't want to talk about this."

"Why not?"

She turned her attention back to the tomato. "Because my sex life is the least of my concerns right now."

He leaned closer. "That's only because you don't have one."

"You could be right." She scraped the tomato wedges off the board and into the salad.

"Anyway, I was asking about basketball," Nick continued casually, as if they hadn't just been talking about intimate matters, "because Ethan and Jake wanted me to convince you to play some two-on-two after dinner."

"I can hardly play basketball dressed like this." She had yet to change out of the skirt and blouse she'd worn to his office earlier.

"I'm sure Kristin has a pair of shorts and a T-shirt you could borrow."

Jess hesitated. Although there had been a time when they would have shared freely one another's wardrobes, it seemed that time had long past.

"Unless you're just looking for an excuse to get out of playing," Nick said.

"Why would I be looking for an excuse?"

He shrugged. "Well, you're not a teenager anymore, and by your own admission, it's been a lot of years since you've played. Don't worry—I'm sure Jake and Ethan will understand that you're not up to it."

It was a subtle but effective challenge. "Who says I'm not up to it?"

Nick started to smile. "Does that mean you'll play?"

"I'll play," she said. "But there's a condition."

His smile faded. "What's the condition?"

"You guys have to do the dishes."

She felt ridiculously nervous as she ran her hands over the surface of the well-worn ball, almost as if it was the beginning of a championship game with NCAA scouts watching instead of a backyard competition with only Katie on the sidelines as their lone spectator and official scorekeeper. Jess had tried to entice the girl to join the game, but Katie seemed more than content to watch the action unfold.

But she knew it wasn't the crowd—or lack thereof—that was making her apprehensive. It was the competition. More specifically: Nick.

He'd been one of those all-around athletes in high school and had played almost everything—soccer, basketball, baseball, football. But football had been his game.

Basketball had been hers.

She didn't doubt that she could still outmaneuver him on the court. What worried her was the possibility of inadvertent body contact as they each vied for control of the ball. Or the possibility that such body contact might not be inadvertent—especially in light of recent revelations about her nonexistent sex life.

It was a crazy thought.

It was a tempting thought.

But she pushed it out of her mind to concentrate on the game.

It was Jess and Ethan against Nick and Jake, and Jess

was determined to give it her all—to make Nick regret even suggesting she wasn't up to this kind of competition.

She crouched in front of him, her eyes on his. She could hear the rhythmic thump of the ball hitting the concrete. She knew where it was, but she was watching the shift of his eyes to anticipate where it was going to be.

And when he pivoted, she darted in, deftly plucking the ball from him and hooking it over her shoulder. It circled around the rim before dropping neatly through the center of the hoop.

"Okay, so you've still got some good moves," he admitted grudgingly.

She flashed him a saucy grin. "You ain't seen nothin' yet."

Jake and Nick rallied for the next point, then Jess and Ethan took three.

The play went back and forth fairly evenly after that, the game both hard fought and fast paced as the score climbed steadily upwards.

She brushed her bangs out of her face and struggled to catch her breath, but she couldn't remember when she'd had more fun. The spirit of the competition was both friendly and fierce, the adrenaline pumping through her veins invigorating and strangely arousing. She'd never known a game of basketball to have that effect on her—then again, she'd usually played with and against other women.

Playing with Nick was a new experience on so many levels. She enjoyed watching him: the way his T-shirt stretched across his broad chest, the flex of the strong muscles in his legs, the sheen of perspiration on his brow, the glint of determination in his blue eyes.

But she was equally determined, and when he managed to steal the ball from her, she responded with a sharp elbow to his ribs. He bobbled the ball, allowing Ethan to sneak in and take it away.

"Ow. Damn." He rubbed his side and glared at Jess. "That was a foul."

She smiled sweetly. "I don't know what you're talking about."

"Katie," Nick called.

But Katie hadn't seen any alleged infraction, because her eyes were glued to Ethan as he jumped up and grabbed the rim for a dunk shot.

"Showoff," Nick grumbled, bending at the waist to catch his breath.

Jess patted his shoulder consolingly. "He's six foot four and seventeen years old. You shouldn't feel…inadequate."

His scowl darkened: "I don't."

And to prove it, he took a pass from his nephew, then feinted to get around Ethan's defense before sending his jump shot home.

Determined not to be outdone, Jess picked up the ball and skirted past him for the layup. Her shot brushed the backboard before dropping through the hoop.

When Nick came back on the return, Jess leapt and managed not just to block his shot but tip it to Ethan, who hooted with laughter as he circled around and went in for another dunk shot.

"And that," Katie called from the sidelines, "is twenty-one."

With a whoop of triumph, Ethan high-fived his partner. Nick collapsed on the driveway while Jake pleaded for a rematch.

Jess dropped down beside Nick, leaned back against his shoulder, her face flushed with pleasure and success.

"Rematch?" he asked.

She glanced at her watch, shook her head. "It's almost eight. I want to make it back up to the hospital tonight, and I'm going to need to hit the shower before I do so."

"Ah, shoot." Jake tossed the ball to Ethan. "I'm stocking shelves at the grocery store tonight and I'm supposed to be there by eight."

"I guess that's my cue to take my ball and go home," Ethan said. He glanced casually in Katie's direction. "Or maybe I'll head to the library—work on my history paper."

"I've got some research to do for a geography project," Katie said. "Mind if I walk over with you?"

"Uh, no."

"Aunt Jess?" Katie turned to her for permission.

As Katie had told her earlier that she'd finished the project, Jess knew it was merely an excuse. Although she wasn't sure if it was an excuse to get out of the house or to be with Ethan. Either way, she didn't see the harm in letting her go—and what authority did she have to refuse, anyway?

"Okay," Jess agreed. "Give me a call when you're finished, and I'll pick you up."

"I can walk her home," Ethan offered, making Jess wonder if his history paper was as bogus as Katie's geography project.

"Okay," she said again. "Thanks."

"Sure."

Katie's smile was blinding. "I'm just going to go in…to grab my books."

"Hmm," was all Nick said when Katie had disappeared back inside the house.

"Hmm, what?"

"That's what I'm trying to figure out," he admitted.

He pushed himself off the concrete, offered a hand to help Jess to her feet. She accepted his assistance gratefully. Although she'd had fun running around with Jake and Ethan, it was humbling to admit—if only to herself—that she was no longer as young or agile as a teenager.

Katie raced out as they were on their way in, saying goodbye with a quick wave.

Jess went straight to the refrigerator, snagged two bottles of water. She tossed one to Nick.

"You looked like you were enjoying yourself out there."

"I was. I did." She smiled. "I almost forgot how much fun it could be."

"And how intense?"

"That, too." She tipped the bottle to her lips, drank deeply.

"What do you know about this geography project of Katie's?" he asked.

She frowned at the abrupt change of topic. "Kristin asked me to remind her about it," she said.

It was the truth, if not the whole truth, and she refused to feel guilty about withholding the fact that Katie had told her she was already finished the project. If Katie and Ethan were sneaking off to the library to spend time together, well, how much trouble could they get into at the library?

"She has a tendency to let things slide," Nick said. "Especially if she's having trouble with something."

"Which only means she's like most other fifteen-year-old girls."

"I heard you've been helping her with her math homework."

Jess nodded. "She's catching on."

"She's a bright kid." But he frowned as he said it.

"Is there a problem?"

"No. Maybe."

"Well, that clarifies things."

He managed a wry smile. "I'm just trying to figure you out."

She finished off her water, recapped the empty bottle and set it aside. "I'm not all that complicated."

"That's what I wanted to believe. Yet every time I turn around, I see a different side of you, and I don't quite know how to put all those pieces together."

She heard the frustration in his voice, and something else, something darker, dangerous.

"You're a bundle of contradictions, Jess. And your being here is slowly driving me insane."

She swallowed. "That certainly isn't my intention."

"Of course not." He set his now half-empty bottle beside hers on the counter and took a step closer to her.

"Nick." It was a plea, a warning.

He ignored her and gently cupped her face in his hands, started to lower his head.

Her breath caught in her throat. His intent was obvious, and although a part of her desperately yearned to feel his mouth on hers, another part—the "been-there-done-that-don't-want-my-heart-broken-again" part—screamed at her to step away, out of the reach of temptation. She fisted her hands, her nails biting into her palms. "Don't kiss me, Nick."

She'd intended to sound decisive, authoritative, but the words were little more than a whisper.

"Why not?"

"Because." She swallowed. "Because it would be a mistake."

"Probably," he agreed, his lips whispering against her cheek. "But not the first one, for either of us."

He teased the corner of her mouth with a feather-light caress, traced the shape of her bottom lip with the tip of his tongue. She felt the warm pulse of desire deep inside, an aching need that spread through her veins, obliterating any lingering protest from the "been-there-done-that" part of her mind.

Her fingers unfurled and her hands lifted to his chest, holding on when she should have been pushing him away. She knew this was a mistake—a mistake they would both regret. But the wanting was stronger than reason.

"And it's a mistake I can't stop myself from making," he said.

Then his mouth covered hers in a long, slow kiss that made everything inside her melt.

Nick had agreed it would be a mistake to kiss her. He'd had no idea how big a mistake until his lips met hers, but he was already past the point of no return.

That first touch, that first taste, destroyed any illusion that he was in control of the moment. Any illusion that he'd ever been in control where Jessica was concerned.

There was a jolt, not unexpected but unexpectedly intense. And there was heat. A lot of heat. Not a slow burning, but a flash explosion. Fiery and powerful and consuming.

He slid his fingers into her hair and tilted her head back to deepen the kiss. Her lips parted willingly to the stroke of his tongue as the passion she'd tried to deny sparked and sizzled between them.

She lifted her arms to wrap around his neck, the soft curves of her body yielding to the hard angles of his.

His hands skimmed over her torso, sliding along the soft cotton of her borrowed T-shirt. He wondered what she was wearing under it. Some dreamy concoction of satin and lace designed to make a man's mouth water? Or something prim and practical?

He realized it didn't matter, because whatever she was wearing, he knew only too well what was beneath. He was intimately familiar with every inch of her. Even after eighteen years, he knew the scent of her soft sweet skin, the feel of her long lean muscles. And he knew how she'd respond to his touch: the way she'd tremble as he stroked her toward the peak of desire, her throaty sighs and murmurs, the fluid arch of her body beneath his. Just as he knew the teasing touch of her lips, the impatient demands of her hands, the welcoming heat of her embrace.

She was soft and she was strong. She was giving and demanding, stubborn and sweet. She was everything he'd ever wanted.

And yes, he wanted her.

But wanting was easy, and if Jessica had given any indication that she was willing, he would have taken her to his bed in a heartbeat. Desire was a simple emotion, and desiring Jess was a given. It was the deeper emotions that went with the desire that continued to tangle him up inside.

He could curse himself for being weak. He could resent the hold she continued to have on him. But he couldn't deny that basic fact that eighteen years later, Jess continued to haunt his thoughts as no other woman ever had.

Was it because she'd made her choices and hadn't chosen him? Could it be that simple? Could he be so shallow as to want her only because she'd once rejected him?

She shifted closer, her breasts rubbing against his chest, and he stopped wondering why he wanted her and simply gave in to the feeling.

He started to slide his hands down his back, reaching for the hem of her T-shirt, when he heard the approach and then the abrupt faltering of footsteps.

He dropped his hands, stepped back.

"Well. I'm, uh, just on my way to work," Jake said. "I'll be back…around midnight." Then he was gone.

Jess glanced at him, then away. Her cheeks were flushed—with passion or embarrassment, he wasn't sure.

"I have to, uh, head up to the hospital."

"Jess."

She hesitated.

"The kiss—you know it was inevitable. It just seemed to me that we should get it out of the way."

"Is it?" she asked softly. "Out of the way?"

His gaze dropped to her mouth, to lips erotically swollen from his kiss. "Hardly."

"Nick…"

"I know I promised we would keep this on the back burner until the situation with Caleb is resolved." And he prayed, for all of their sakes, it would be soon. "But I think what just happened between us proves we can't let it simmer for too long."

A long uncomfortable silence hung between them. Then Jessica sighed and turned to leave. "I'll see you at your office in the morning." She exited the room.

Nick knew he should leave, too. He still had to make some changes to the blueprints Mason had dropped off earlier and there were a dozen other little things to take care of for the business. Things he hadn't managed to do earlier that day because he'd been aware of and preoccupied with Jessica's presence in his office.

Instead, he leaned back against the counter and picked up his drink. He heard the water running through the pipes overhead, knew she was getting ready to step into the shower.

It was all too easy to imagine how she'd look as she stripped away the T-shirt and shorts she'd been wearing, stepped under the warm spray. The water would slide over the strong line of her shoulders, over the curve of her creamy breasts, the flat stomach, down her long legs. He cursed the vivid mental image, and his own body for responding so predictably.

It had been eighteen years since they'd been together. Eighteen years after only one night together. And yet he'd never forgotten anything about her.

He downed the last of the cool water, but it failed to chill the heat coursing through his veins. Cursing himself and his masochistic tendencies, he stalked out of the house.

Jessica made what was intended to be a quick stop at the bookstore on her way to the hospital, but when she walked into Caleb's room her arms were groaning with the weight of the bags she was carrying.

"What's all that?" Kristin asked.

She dumped the books and magazines onto the ledge, then began sorting them into two piles.

"Some new books for Caleb," she said, setting them on the small table beside his bed and bending to press a soft kiss to his cheek. "Because I'm sure he's getting tired of hearing the same stories over and over again."

Then she turned back to Kristin. "And some magazines for you."

Kristin took the stack she held out, flipped through to look at the covers. "They're design and decorating magazines."

"I remembered that you wanted to go to college to become an interior designer."

"Yeah, like ten years ago."

Jess's smile slipped. "I can go back to the bookstore if you'd prefer something else."

"No," Kristin said. "These are fine. I'm just surprised that you remembered."

"It was your house that reminded me. You did a great job with the colors and fabrics."

Kristin shrugged. "I had fun picking everything out."

"It shows. I should have you come to New York and do my condo."

"I'm hardly a professional."

"I had a professional," Jess admitted. "He painted everything white. It's stark and cold and horrible."

"If you hate it so much, why didn't you change it?"

"I'm not really there that much, and when I am, I'm usually sleeping." She shrugged and lowered herself into the vacant chair beside Kristin. "But I'd love it if you wanted to come down sometime and check it out. See if you have any ideas."

"Really?" Her friend sounded pleased, if surprised, by the comment.

"Of course."

"Maybe I will," Kristin said. "After everything's back to normal."

"Any news on when that might be?" she asked gently.

Kristin only shook her head.

"Can I ask a question?"

"Sure."

"If being an interior designer was something you really wanted, why didn't you go back to school?"

Her friend sighed. "The time just never seemed right. And now, well, I think I'm a little too old to be starting college."

"You're only ten months older than me," Jess reminded her dryly. "And we're not old. But even so, I don't think it's ever too late to go after a dream."

"Dreams change."

"Sometimes," she agreed.

"I was going to do it," Kristin admitted after a pause, "when Katie started school full-time. I had the college calendar, my courses all picked out. Then I got pregnant with Caleb."

And, suddenly, her eyes filled with tears.

Before Jess could question her further, Kristin changed the subject.

"Jake stopped by on his way into work," she said. "He told me that he and Ethan conned you and Nick into playing basketball with them."

"Yeah." She shifted in her chair, tucking one foot beneath her. "I felt guilty, playing around while you were here with Caleb—"

"Don't apologize," Kristin said. "I was happy to hear that the kids were having fun, that they could pretend—if only for a little while—that life was normal.

"This has been so hard on everyone, but especially Jake. He's so much like Brian, the way he keeps everything bottled up inside."

Jess nodded.

"I'm glad you're spending time with them."

"I'm enjoying being with them."

"And Nick?" Kristin prompted.

She tensed. "What about Nick?"

"Jake told me that he saw you and Nick kissing."

"Jake sure was talkative tonight," Jess grumbled.

Kristin managed a smile. "He likes to control the conversation so I can't ask about Becky."

"Who's Becky?"

"Jake's ex-girlfriend. They dated for almost a year, then she dumped him for some college guy."

"I don't think he's pining for her."

Kristin's interest was obviously piqued. "Why do you say that?"

"Because he spent an hour on the phone last night with someone named Lara."

"Really? Did he tell you anything about her?"

"Only that she was in his biology class. But his ears turned pink when I asked."

Kristin smiled again. "That's a definite sign he's interested."

"I remember that Brian's ears used to turn pink whenever you said 'hello' to him in the halls."

The smile faded. "That was a lifetime ago."

"He still looks at you the way he did back then."

She shook her head.

But it was the abject sadness that filled her eyes that changed Jess's gentle teasing to concern. "Kris?"

"You've managed to distract me and avoid answering my original question about Nick."

"I don't remember you asking one."

"Were you and my brother kissing in the kitchen?"

"Yes," Jess admitted reluctantly. "But it was nothing more than a moment of insanity."

"For you or him?"

"For both of us."

Kristin was silent for a minute before asking, "Are you ever going to tell me what happened between the two of you?"

"It's ancient history."

"Is it?" Then, before Jess could respond, she continued. "I've noticed the way you tiptoe around each other. The way you've tiptoed around each other for years. You used to be friends—good friends—and I can't figure out when that changed, or why."

She knew Kristin was waiting for an explanation. She wondered if there was some way to answer the question without revealing the whole truth, but immediately discarded the thought. There had been too many secrets and evasions already, and she didn't think their friendship could survive any more. She didn't *want* there to be any more. She wanted her best friend back, and she knew that could only happen if she finally told her the truth about what had happened so many years ago.

"It changed because we had sex," she admitted.

She thought Kristin would be surprised, shocked even. But her friend merely nodded.

"I always thought so," she said. "Considering how close the two of you were, it almost seemed inevitable. Now my question is, what went wrong?"

This truth was a lot harder to admit, and she avoided her friend's gaze as she whispered, "I got pregnant."

Chapter Seven

"Pregnant?" The shock was evident in her friend's voice.

Jessica bit down on her lip and nodded.

"What happened?" Kristin asked softly.

"I had—" she swallowed around the tightness in her throat "—a miscarriage."

"Oh, Jess."

She managed a shrug. But after so many years, her feelings about the loss were anything but casual. "In retrospect, it was probably for the best. I was just seventeen and Nick wasn't much older. We were little more than kids ourselves. We had no business even thinking about being parents."

"But you wanted the baby."

She should have known Kristin would understand. Kristin had *always* understood. And she regretted again that she'd kept such a huge secret from her best friend for so long. But at the time she'd been so confused about her relationship with Nick that she didn't even know how she felt, never mind how Kristin would feel about her best friend being involved with her brother.

She nodded. "I know it sounds crazy, but yeah—I did."

"And Nick would have, too," Kristin assured her. "He's always wanted a bunch of kids."

She nodded again.

Kristin touched her arm. "I'm so sorry, Jess."

"I wanted to tell you…" She felt the sting of tears as she remembered how desperately she'd wanted to tell Kristin, how much she'd needed her best friend's understanding and compassion. But it had hurt too much to talk about it with anyone.

"I know it must have been hard for both of you," Kristin said gently. "But I would have thought something like that would bring you closer together, not push you apart."

"I don't understand it, either," Jess admitted. "At the time, when I tried to talk to him about the miscarriage, he was so cold and distant." Nothing like the man who'd held her in his arms and told her he loved her.

Kristin frowned. "That doesn't sound like my brother."

Jess could only shrug, her throat tight.

Losing Nick had hurt even more than losing her baby, not just because they'd shared so much history but because they'd planned for a future together. Then she'd miscarried and he'd dropped out of her life completely.

"Have you talked to him about it since then?" Kristin asked.

"I—I couldn't."

"Jess." It was both a sigh and a reprimand.

She only sighed. "I know. I will."

But at the time she'd been so devastated she hadn't been

able to gather the pieces of her broken heart to confront him about what had happened. Maybe it was past time that she did so.

"In the meantime," Kristin continued, "there's obviously still an attraction between you."

She smiled wryly. "An attraction, maybe. But nothing more than that."

"Are you sure?"

"We had a brief fling eighteen years ago. We've hardly spoken since then, so I'd have to say, yes, I'm sure." But though her words sounded convincing, her heart was less certain.

"I'm sorry I pressured you to help out in Nick's office."

Jess shrugged. "It's not a big deal."

"The thing is, I figured something had happened between the two of you," Kristin admitted. "And I was hoping that by forcing you together, you might somehow work it out."

"I think it's going to take more than my questionable secretarial skills to do that."

When Brian stopped by the hospital later that night, he was surprised to find that Kristin wasn't in Caleb's room. He didn't think she'd left his bedside since their son had been brought in, but she wasn't there now. Instead, it was Jessica sitting beside Caleb's bed, reading to him.

The tension that had been building inside him as he prepared for yet another confrontation with his wife eased somewhat, to be immediately replaced by guilt that he was glad she wasn't there.

Kristin had seemed surprised that Jess had dropped everything to come to Pinehurst when she'd learned of the accident. He wasn't. He knew that Kristin and Jessica shared a lot of history, and this was the type of tragedy that helped bridge distances.

Weddings and funerals—beginnings and endings—two occasions that never failed to bring old friends and distant family together again.

He glanced across the room at his youngest child, who had only just begun to live. The accident had left few visible marks on his skin and he looked as though he was sleeping. It was only the incessant dripping of tubes, the steady hissing and blipping of machines that hinted of his struggle between life and death.

Please God, don't let this end with a funeral.

He didn't know how he could survive if Caleb didn't.

And Kristin—the kids were her life. Jake and Katie and Caleb, they were her reason for being. The source of all her joys and frustrations. And now, her pain.

He was glad Jessica was here. He hoped that she would be able to help Kristin in some small way, even if just to provide a distraction.

"That was one of my favorites as a kid," he told Jess, gesturing to the book in her hands.

"Mine, too." She closed the cover, set it aside. "Kristin just went down to the chapel, but I can go find her—"

He shook his head. "I'm glad she's finally let herself take a break, even if only for a few minutes."

He picked up some kind of decorating magazine that had been left on the other chair, moved it aside. "Kristin hasn't bought one of these in years."

"I brought it in," Jess admitted. "I remembered that she'd once expressed an interest in studying interior design."

"Did she?" It was news to Brian.

"A long time ago." She smiled ruefully. "Shows you how out of touch I've been."

Or maybe he was the one who was out of touch. "She used to talk about going back to school, but she hasn't said anything about it in years."

Then again, he and Kristin didn't seem capable of communication these days, not beyond the most basic exchanges of information concerning his work schedule and the kids' various activities. Anything more invariably degenerated into an argument.

"I imagine the kids keep her busy."

He nodded. "She's always running them from one place to another—ballet, swimming, cub scouts. And she does volunteer work, taking a turn as lunchroom monitor at the high school, helping—" he heard his voice break, cleared his throat "—helping in Caleb's classroom."

Jess reached over and squeezed his hand. "He'll be back at school before you know it."

"Yeah." But he knew he sounded more desperate than optimistic.

"I hardly recognized him when I came in yesterday," she admitted to him. "The last time I saw him, he was a toddler on chubby legs with less hair than you have now."

He managed to smile at her teasing, rubbed a hand over the shortly shorn hair on his scalp. "And it probably wasn't gray."

"No." She brushed a lock of blond hair off of Caleb's forehead. "I didn't realize so much time had passed."

"When was your last visit home?"

"July, six years ago," she said. "I came back for Kristin's mom's funeral."

Weddings and funerals, he thought again, and pushed the thought aside.

* * *

When Nick got home, he locked himself in the office and turned his attention to the blueprints Mason had dropped off earlier, resolutely blocking all thoughts of Jessica from his mind.

At least, he tried to.

But when the lines on the page started to blur together, he found his mind drifting. And when he finally gave up and went to sleep, he dreamed of her. Remembering in his sleep what he wouldn't allow himself to think about while he was awake. Remembering the night they'd made love.

It was the night of Kristin and Brian's wedding, after the guests had all gone home.

He'd been feeling restless, edgy, and decided to take a walk out through the woods behind his parents' home. He'd been feeling edgy all day, from the moment he'd first spotted Jessica at the back of the church.

She was wearing a strapless gown of pale blue silk. The material was snug around the bodice, emphasizing the swell of her breasts and the narrowness of her waist before falling in an elegant column to her ankles. But it wasn't the dress so much as the woman in it who stole his breath.

Her long dark had been swept up off the back of her neck into some kind of fancy twist. Her gorgeous whiskey-colored eyes had been dramatically highlighted and the soft curve of her lips painted a glossy shade of pink.

As he watched her glide up the aisle, he tried to remember that she was only seventeen years old. But she didn't look like a teenager. She looked like a fantasy—his fantasy.

In that fantasy, he would pluck the pins from her hair and bury his hands in the cascade of curls, tip her head back to devour that luscious mouth, then strip away the barrier of silk to run his hands over those delectable curves, and finally fit his body intimately with hers.

The fantasy was vivid in his mind; the punch of desire staggering. And in church, no less. He would surely burn in hell for the thoughts that were running through his mind, but even that certainty couldn't rein in his lustful thoughts.

Still, he'd managed to keep his hands off her by maintaining a careful distance between them throughout the evening. At least until he stepped through the trees and saw her standing in the moonlight.

Then she'd asked him to dance, and he'd been unable to refuse. In that moment, he couldn't have refused her anything. And when he'd taken her in his arms, it was so much better than any fantasy.

Then he'd kissed her. Just the slightest brush of his lips against hers; just a taste of temptation. He'd promised himself that one kiss would be enough. But then she slid her arms around his neck, helped him deepen the kiss.

The unexpected passion in her response almost destroyed the last vestiges of his self-control. Almost.

Somehow he managed to ease his lips from hers, pull away. "You need to tell me to stop, Jessica."

She looked up at him, her eyes dark with passion, her lips erotically swollen from their kiss, and asked, "Why?"

"Because I don't have enough willpower to walk away on my own."

It was a plea for her to be smarter than he was, stronger than he was. A plea she immediately rejected.

"I don't want you to walk away."

And so he didn't. He couldn't.

He couldn't do anything but lower his head to kiss her again.

His hands found the zipper at the back of her dress, slid it downward as his mouth cruised down the column of her throat, then lower, to the curve of pale creamy flesh above the lace-edged cup of her bra. She shivered, just a quick little tremor that he found unbearably arousing. Then again, everything about Jess was proving to be unbearably arousing.

He felt the urgency building inside, tamped it down. He wanted to savor every inch of her and every minute of their first time together. Ruthlessly restraining his own growing desire, he explored her slowly, thoroughly, with his hands and his lips.

Her soft sighs turned to throaty moans, her hesitant explorations turned to urgent demands. She arched and wrapped herself around him. Desire gave way to passion; want to need.

Finally, when he could hold back no longer, when she was no longer satisfied with touching and kissing, he parted her thighs and drove into her slick heat.

She gasped, her eyes went wide with shock, pain, and her muscles clenched so tight around him he thought he might explode. He was grasping with a slippery fist for the little bit of control he had left. He held himself immobile, only dipping his head to move his lips over hers, slowly, coaxingly. Slowly the tension seeped out of her body and her hips lifted to accommodate his entry. Now she sighed and locked her endlessly long legs around his waist to pull him even deeper inside.

This time it was Nick who moaned as her body began to move with his in a timeless and instinctive rhythm. It was lust that drove him to possess her; love that tempered his *possession. Because he did love her, had always loved her, would always love her. Just as he knew that she wouldn't be here with him now if she didn't love him, too. In that moment, he vowed that he wouldn't only be her first, he would be her last—her forever.*

He felt the tension building inside her again, but it was a different tension this time. He watched as her eyes glazed over, felt her tremble, shudder, and swallowed her stunned cry as she tumbled over the precipice, taking him with her.

Jess glanced at her watch, knocked again, harder this time. She knew she was early, but Nick had said he was usually in the office by eight and though it was almost eight-thirty, the door was still locked.

His vehicle—she knew now that it was his—was in the driveway, so obviously he was home. Maybe he was on the phone. Or maybe he'd gone back to the house for something.

She hesitated a moment then finally moved to the main entrance, pressed the bell. After a minute, she pressed it a second time. At last she heard what she thought sounded like footsteps.

The door pulled open abruptly and Nick was there, glaring at her through bleary eyes, his hair still tousled from sleep, his jaw dark with golden stubble.

Inadvertently, her gaze slipped down past his face, her mind registering the fact that he wasn't wearing anything but a pair of navy, plaid pajama bottoms.

Her mouth went dry.

Okay, coming to the house was obviously a bad idea. But while her brain warned her to retreat, she couldn't stop herself from taking a more leisurely perusal. Over broad shoulders, across a firmly muscled chest, down the rippling abs to an arrowing of dark blond hair that dipped into the front of his pajama bottoms.

"What the hell are you doing here?"

She felt a guilty flush infuse her cheeks, forced her gaze back to his. "I, uh, told you I'd come in early today. To catch up on the filing."

He scrubbed a hand over his jaw. "I didn't realize you meant at the crack of dawn."

"It's almost eight-thirty."

He swore again. "Amber never sleeps through the alarm."

"Oh." She felt her cheeks flush as the impact of his response hit. Amber was obviously the reason he was looking so tired and tousled this morning. "Well, I, uh, didn't mean to intrude. If you wouldn't mind unlocking the office, I can go in and get started."

"Or you could come in and make coffee," he said, turning away from the door as if he expected her to follow. "I have a feeling I'm going to need a gallon of it to get through the day."

"That's not part of my job description," she said coolly.

She had no intention of making coffee for Nick and Amber. Not that he didn't have every right to sleep with whoever he wanted, whenever he wanted, she just didn't want to be a witness to any of their morning-after intimacies.

"I'm in a pissy mood this morning, Jess. If you don't want to make coffee, fine. I'll get you the key to the office."

Reluctantly she followed him into the house, hoping Amber was still discreetly tucked away in his bedroom. She wasn't prepared to make nice with Nick's latest girl-friend. Not that she had any residual feelings for him, just that it was inevitably awkward when a former lover came face-to-face with the current one.

He opened a tall cupboard, the hinges creaking slightly.

Jess started as a sleek yellow tabby cat suddenly came bounding into the kitchen, rubbing up against Nick's leg, meowing plaintively.

"You're awake now, are you? Lazy cat." Despite his muttering, he reached down and rubbed his knuckles gently over the top of the cat's head.

Now she had an entirely different reason to feel embarrassed. "Is that, uh, Amber?"

"That's Amber," he agreed, handing her the key he'd retrieved from the cupboard.

"I didn't know you had a cat." And what kind of name was Amber for a cat, anyway?

"Katie found her, abandoned in a shoebox as a kitten, but Brian's allergic so she brought it here." Then he looked up at her, understanding—and a hint of amusement—glinting in his eyes. "You thought Amber was a woman."

"It was a natural conclusion to draw," she said defensively.

"Natural—why?"

"Because you came to the door wearing only half of your pajamas, obviously annoyed that I'd interrupted…something."

"Yeah—my sleep."

He moved to another cupboard, pulled out a box of coffee filters, a tin of coffee. "Did you really think I would have kissed you the way I did last night and then taken someone else to my bed?"

She lifted a shoulder, deliberately casual. "That's really none of my business, is it?"

"Not every man plays musical women like your ex-husband."

Ouch. "I know that. But it's not as if we have any kind of, uh, relationship."

"No," he agreed after a long moment. "I guess we don't."

"Nick?"

"Yeah."

"You're still only half-dressed."

"So?"

"So, I'd appreciate it if you'd, uh, put some clothes on."

"My mornings have a certain order to them," he told her. "And coffee comes before anything else."

She took the carafe to fill it from the tap. "I'll make it."

"It's not in your job description," he reminded her.

"That's when I thought I was making it for you and Amber." She dumped the water into the reservoir. "I have no objection to making coffee for…a friend."

"Is that what we are, Jess—friends?"

"We used to be," she said softly.

"Yeah." He scrubbed his hand over his jaw. "I'm going to shower."

She nodded, wondering why every time they started to talk about something that mattered, one or the other of them abruptly changed the topic.

She was halfway through her first cup of coffee when Nick came back down the stairs.

He was freshly showered and dressed, in softly faded jeans and a plain navy polo shirt that emphasized the deep blue of his eyes. Her heart skipped a beat and she wondered, with no small amount of frustration, if he would always have this effect on her, as if she'd never gotten over her teenage crush.

"Feel better?" she asked lightly.

"No." He poured himself a cup of coffee, started to carry it to the table, then doubled back to retrieve something from inside the cupboard. He settled down at the opposite side of the table, pushed a key across the table to her. "There. Go."

"You are in a pissy mood this morning."

"Yeah, I am. And you'd be smart to take that key and get out of here."

"Is there a particular reason you're angry with me, or has all of this just been building over the past eighteen years?"

"Both." He took a long swallow from his mug.

"Are you going to explain that cryptic comment?"

His eyes locked on hers, dark and dangerous. "I dreamed about you last night. About making love with you."

All of the air rushed out of her lungs. "Oh."

His lips turned up in a rueful half smile. "Do you still want me to tell you about it?"

"I, uh, that's probably not necessary."

"Probably not," he agreed. "You don't need the details to know I want you in my bed again."

There it was—straight out. No frills, no pretty words, no promises. Not that she wanted or expected any of those things from Nick, nor did she expect to be treated as if she was a piece of prime meat at the butcher shop.

"Well, then," she said coolly, "show me to your bedroom so we can get to it."

This time, there was genuine humor in his smile. And it irked her that even though she was justifiably angry with him, the slow curve of his lips still made her knees weak.

"Now you're mad."

"I guess you know me better than you thought."

Yeah, she was mad, he noted. But the darkening of her eyes hinted at something more.

He nodded. "Angry. Annoyed. And just a little bit tempted."

"Tempted to dump my coffee over your head."

Instead, she carried her mug to the sink, dumped it there.

"I may have kissed you last night, but you kissed me back," he reminded her.

She shrugged. "I was curious."

"You were a hell of a lot more than curious."

He drained the last of his coffee, rose from the table for a refill. Then he decided he didn't want caffeine as much as he wanted Jess, and he pushed the mug aside, turning so he'd trapped her between himself and the counter.

"In fact—" he lifted one of his hands to cup her cheek, saw by the pulse beating at the base of her jaw that her heart rate had quickened "—if Jake hadn't come into the kitchen, who knows what might have happened?"

"*Nothing* would have happened."

He brushed his thumb over the tempting curve of her bottom lip. "Now I'm going to have to test that theory," he warned.

"I thought we agreed to put this aside until later."

His lips brushed against hers.

Once.

Twice.

"It is later," he said.

Then again.

If she'd pulled back, he would have released her. If she'd made any kind of protest or shown any resistance, he would have stepped away.

But when his mouth touched hers again, she merely sighed and sank with him into the kiss.

Her lips parted eagerly to the searching thrust of his tongue. She wrapped her arms around him, pressed her body against his. His hands raced over her, greedy and demanding, wanting not just to touch, but to possess. Needing her as he'd never needed another woman.

His heart pounded in a primitive rhythm as he tugged her shirt out of her pants. Then his hands were on her skin, stroking over the heated flesh. He felt her tremble in response to his touch, swallowed her throaty moan of pleasure.

Everything about the kiss was exactly as he'd remembered. Her taste. Her touch. Her passion. And it was more than he'd remembered. More than he'd wanted. More than he'd been prepared for. More—and still not nearly enough.

That was how it had always been—him wanting more than Jessica could give. It was this realization that helped him ease away from her.

She stared at him, her slightly parted lips erotically swollen from his kisses, her whiskey-colored eyes still dark with passion.

"Nick?"

Just his name, in that soft breathless whisper, and he wanted only to reach for her again, to finish what they hadn't even begun. He knew he could take her, right here in his kitchen, braced against the counter, on the hard butcher's block table, or the cold tile floor—it wouldn't matter. They both wanted the same thing: to quench the fire that raged inside them.

But he ignored the demands of his aching body and took a careful step back. He saw the passion in her eyes fade to confusion, then hurt, as he deliberately moved away from her.

"I wanted to forgive you," he said. "I really tried to forgive you. But after all this time, I still can't get past what you did."

"What *I* did?" There was confusion again, then her temper sparked. "It's not as if I was trying to get pregnant."

"I know," he agreed. "And I was willing to accept full responsibility for that. Hell, Jess, I even offered to marry you." He couldn't look at her now, so he turned to refill his mug with coffee he no longer wanted. "You were the one who decided your scholarship was more important than our baby."

She gasped. "How can you even suggest something like that?"

"It's the truth."

"*Nothing* was more important to me than our baby."

She spoke with such anguished conviction, he almost believed her. Which only proved he'd always been a sucker where Jess was concerned.

"Then why did you get rid of it?" he demanded, facing her again.

He saw the moment that confusion gave way to comprehension. Her face, flushed with passion only moments before, paled. "Y-you think I had…an…abortion?"

His righteous anger faltered, but only for a second. Because he wasn't wrong about this. "I *know* you did."

She shook her head fiercely, her eyes filled with tears. "I would never—"

He couldn't listen to any more denials. He couldn't let her tears weaken his conviction in the truth. "I know," he said again, "because your mother told me."

Chapter Eight

Jess stumbled back, as if each of his words was a physical blow. An attack she couldn't block, could never have anticipated.

Eighteen years after she'd lost her baby, and then her baby's father, she'd never thought anything could hurt as much. This came close.

Lillian Harding had come as soon as she'd learned her daughter was in the hospital. She'd held her hand, offered comfort and support, promised everything would be okay. Then, with a few deliberately chosen words, she'd made sure nothing would ever be okay again.

No, Jess refused to believe it. There was no way that her mother would ever tell Nick such lies. She just wouldn't.

And yet, the first seeds of doubt were planted in the back of her mind.

It had been her mother's dream as much as her own for

Jess to get out of Pinehurst. To go to college, have a real career. She wanted her daughter to have the kind of life she'd once dreamed of—a dream eclipsed by her own unplanned pregnancy.

Was it possible her own mother had sabotaged any hope Jess had of a future with Nick? No, Jess couldn't believe it. Her mother had never wanted anything but the best for Jessica. She would never hurt her in such a way.

From somewhere in the distance, she heard Nick swear, then felt his hand gripping her arm. He pressed a glass of water into her other hand.

"Drink."

Her mind was too busy trying to accept his revelation to do anything but obey. She tipped the cup to her mouth, swallowed.

"Jess?"

He was peering at her intently, concerned despite the waves of anger she could still feel rolling off of him.

"She wouldn't have said that," Jess said weakly.

"She did. Why are you surprised? Did you tell her to lie to me about what really happened?"

"No!" She was shocked that he would even suggest such a thing. That he could believe she'd abort their baby then claim it was a miscarriage. "Of course not."

But she could see the stark pain beneath the fury in his eyes, and she knew that he believed what he was saying.

In that moment, everything made sense. His distance. His bitterness. His hostility. And even as her mind cursed him for his lack of faith in her, her heart ached for him.

"Nick—"

"I don't want to talk about it anymore, Jess." He dropped her arm. "I know you probably believed it was the best option. I just can't forgive you for making that decision on your own."

She felt the coldness of despair deep in her heart as she realized he'd accepted this lie as truth, and he'd hated her for it. She didn't know how to get past that, how to make him listen to her, she only knew that she couldn't let him continue to believe something that wasn't true.

"I don't care if you don't want to talk about it," she said. "It's past time for the truth to come out."

He turned away.

Jess moved over to the counter, stood so that she was toe-to-toe with him. "Maybe you don't know me anymore. But you know who I was eighteen years ago. And you know, in your heart, that I couldn't have had…" She trailed off, unable to even say the word *abortion* again.

"I wanted our baby, Nick. Because it was a part of me and you, and because I loved you." She felt the sting of fresh tears, willed them not to fall. "But on September twenty-second, in the middle of my first year English lit course, my appendix burst. I had emergency surgery, but I still lost the baby.

"If you want me to sign a medical release so you can see the hospital records, I will. Because I can't let you go on believing that I purposely got rid of our child."

Blinded as she was by the tears in her eyes, she wasn't sure how she managed to find the door. But she did, and she walked out with her head held high.

Nick let her go.

Still reeling from the enormity of what she'd told him, he didn't even try to stop her. He'd been hurt and angry for so long, he didn't know how to let go of those emotions.

All these years, he'd believed that Jess was responsible for the sense of loss he'd carried with him from that day. But even though it was hard accepting what she'd told him, she was right—in his heart, he knew the truth. And he damned himself for not seeing it eighteen years ago.

They'd both been so young, so naively optimistic about their future together. They were going to get married, raise their baby together, have more babies.

Jessica, he remembered now, hadn't quite shared his level of enthusiasm.

"I don't want you to resent me and the baby for tying you down."

He understood the root of her fear.

"I'm not your father, Jess."

"I know you're not. But the circumstances—"

"Are completely different," he insisted. *"Because I love you."*

Her beautiful eyes filled with tears.

"I've never thought of this baby as a mistake, only as an opportunity."

"Do you really believe that?"

"I really do."

"Promise me that we can make this work. Promise me that you won't ever leave me."

"I won't ever leave you, Jess. Even when we can't be together, you're always in my heart."

"Promise me," she said again.

"I promise."

But he'd broken that promise.

It wasn't an excuse to say that he'd only done so because he was hurting—not when he now knew how much she'd been hurting, too. He'd promised to always be there, and yet, when she'd needed him most, he'd turned away.

Again, even now when she'd asked him for nothing more than acceptance and understanding, he'd refused. Because he couldn't acknowledge the truth was different than what he'd believed for so long. Because he'd spent the better part of so many years blaming her for everything that had gone wrong between them.

When the truth was, he was at fault.

He'd believed the lie her mother told him when he should have loved and trusted Jessica enough to know that she would never make such a choice. Certainly not without talking to him about it first.

He scrubbed his hands over his face as an even more painful truth became clear. He'd believed the lies because he'd wanted to believe them. Because he'd been twenty years old and unprepared for the commitment of marriage and parenthood. He had loved Jessica and he'd been willing to marry her and be a father to their child. Willing— but not ready.

As devastated as he'd been to learn that their baby was gone, he'd also been relieved. And then he'd felt guilty for feeling relieved, so he'd blamed everything on Jessica.

He'd never asked for an explanation or given her a chance to explain. Because he hadn't wanted to understand, he'd only wanted distance. Distance from Jessica and the broken promise of a future that had both enticed and terrified him.

He grabbed his keys. He needed to find her, to finally finish the conversation they should have had eighteen years earlier.

He was reaching for the door handle of his Explorer

when another vehicle pulled into the driveway. He cursed under his breath as he recognized Mason's Acura.

"You finished with the Stilwell project?" Mason asked through the open window, turning off the engine.

It took Nick a minute to clear all the other thoughts from his mind and focus on the question. Stilwell. Renovations. He nodded. He'd completed the changes last night, before he'd gone to sleep and been tormented by dreams of Jessica.

"They're on my desk. You can go in and grab them. I'm on my way out."

"Are you going to the hospital? Has there been any news about your nephew?"

Christ, he hadn't even spoken to Kristin today to know. Since Caleb's accident, he'd been in the habit of stopping by the hospital first thing each morning or at least calling if he couldn't do so. Today, he'd been so wrapped up with Jessica and his own feelings about everything that had happened between him, he hadn't thought of anything else.

"No, I—" He faltered, because the truth was, he had no idea where he was going. His only thought had been to find Jessica. Although it occurred to him now that she would probably have gone to the hospital, and the hospital was hardly the appropriate place to continue their conversation.

"I just have some errands to run," he told Mason.

"Do you think you could stop by the Stilwells on your way back? Nadine is eager to discuss some of the changes with you."

He sighed. "Yesterday's changes or new changes?"

"I don't know. But I know that she was very clear in wanting to deal directly with you."

The news didn't surprise Nick. He was sure one of the reasons they'd been given the Stilwell's renovation contract was because the new Mrs. Stilwell had been involved with Mason prior to meeting and marrying her husband. But he couldn't figure out if Nadine had chosen Armstrong & Sullivan because she still had favorable feelings toward Mason or because she wanted to torment him with the fact that she was no longer available.

Considering the hoops they'd been jumping through since taking on this project, Nick guessed her intention was torment. And as it was a potentially lucrative project, he was prepared to jump through his share of those hoops— he only wished it didn't have to be today.

"All right." He glanced at his watch, figured the time it would take to check in with Kristin at the hospital and then swing by the Stilwells. "You can tell Nadine I'll be there around noon."

"Thanks." Mason turned toward the house. "I'll just grab the blueprints and take a few minutes to flirt with your secretary before I head back there."

"Jess isn't in the office."

"Oh." He hesitated. "Did you screw it up already?"

Nick scowled but couldn't deny it.

"That's where you were going—to grovel."

He wouldn't have put it in those terms, but he supposed Mason's assessment was accurate. If he had any hope of making things right, he was going to have to do some major groveling.

But he had other obligations and responsibilities to deal with first. The conversation with Jessica had already waited eighteen years, it could wait another few hours.

And maybe during those few hours he could somehow find the words to undo the damage that had been done so many years before.

* * *

"You've been crying."

It was the first thing Kristin said when Jess walked into Caleb's room.

So much for cold compresses and cosmetics, she thought, but she forced a smile. "Good morning to you, too."

Then she turned away from her friend's penetrating gaze to focus on the child who still lay motionless in his narrow bed, his skin pale against the white sheets. "And how's our big guy this morning?"

"No change," Kristin said. "The doctor wants to do some more tests today."

"It hasn't been that long," Jess said gently. "He probably just needs some time to heal."

"I wish I could believe that's all it was." Her eyes filled with tears, but she valiantly blinked them back. "I'm guessing," she continued, "since you're here and not at my brother's office, that you've resumed your campaign of avoidance."

"Actually, I was at Nick's office already this morning."

"He's the reason for the tears?" Kristin guessed.

"Not Nick so much as the situation," Jess told her.

"The situation then or now?"

"Then *and* now." She felt the sting of tears in her own eyes again, wished she could be as strong as Kristin. "I didn't come here to talk to you about this. You have enough things to worry about."

"Please," Kristin said. "Tell me. Give me something else to think about."

Jess managed a small smile. "Well, we finally talked about what happened—with the baby." The tears she'd refused to shed in front of Nick couldn't be held back from her best friend. "He thought I had an abortion."

Get FREE BOOKS and a FREE GIFT when you play the...

LAS VEGAS

GAME

*Just scratch off
the gold box with a coin.
Then check below to see
the gifts you get!*

YES! I have scratched off the gold box. Please send me my **2 FREE BOOKS** and **gift for which I qualify**. I understand that I am under no obligation to purchase any books as explained on the back of this card.

335 SDL D7XM   235 SDL D7YN

FIRST NAME   LAST NAME

ADDRESS

APT.#   CITY

STATE/PROV.   ZIP/POSTAL CODE   (S-SE-10/05)

7	7	7	Worth TWO FREE BOOKS plus a BONUS Mystery Gift!
🍒	🍒	🍒	Worth TWO FREE BOOKS!
🔔	🔔	♣	TRY AGAIN!

www.eHarlequin.com

Offer limited to one per household and not valid to current Silhouette Special Edition® subscribers. All orders subject to approval.

Kristin looked as stunned as Jess had felt when Nick had thrown out the accusation. "Why would he think that?"

"Because apparently that's what my mother told him."

This time it was Kristin who took her hand, a silent gesture of support.

"I didn't believe him at first. I didn't want to believe she would make up such a lie. Then I realized that whether she used the actual word or he misunderstood what she was telling him, what matters is that he believed it to be true."

"Oh, Jess."

She felt the sting of fresh tears. "It certainly explains a lot of things."

"I guess it does, except for what happens now."

"There is no 'now.'"

"If that was true," her friend pointed out gently, "this wouldn't still hurt so much."

Jess wiped the tears from her cheeks. "Maybe not."

"Did you tell him what really happened?"

She nodded. "At this point, I'm not sure it matters, but I didn't want him to continue believing a lie."

"It matters." His voice was thick with emotion.

She started, her teary gaze flying to the doorway where Nick stood.

He walked toward her, his steady blue gaze locked with hers. "Of course it matters, Jess."

She swallowed.

"Then maybe you should have talked to her about it eighteen years ago," Kristin said, surprising Jess by coming to her defense.

"Yeah, I should have." He stepped into the room, bent to kiss his scowling sister's cheek. "I'm hoping she'll talk to me about it now."

"I wouldn't blame her if she wouldn't."

"You're both talking about me as if I'm not in the room," Jess pointed out.

"Sorry," Kristin said. "But I can't help thinking that a lot of this miscommunication could have been avoided if at least one of you had talked to me about this when it happened.

"I know," she continued when Jess opened her mouth to speak, "you didn't want me to get caught in the middle. But since I'm there now, I'm going to insist you listen to this hardheaded idiot."

"This isn't the time or the place," Jess began.

"No, it isn't," Nick agreed.

"After eighteen years, it's past time," Kristin said. "And there's a visitor's lounge next door where you can have some privacy."

"Jess?" Nick asked.

She was feeling too raw to get into it right now, but she also didn't want to argue with him in front of Kristin, so she nodded and followed him out of the room.

Nick pulled the door of the lounge shut before he said, "I'm sorry."

She had to ask. "Sorry I lost the baby? Or sorry you didn't trust me?"

"Both."

She fell silent.

"You have every right to be angry."

Jess walked over to the window, peered out at the gray September sky. "I'm not angry."

"Then what are you feeling?"

"I don't know," she admitted. "I can't figure out whether I'm numb or just empty."

She turned back to face him folding her arms across her

chest. "I was angry at first," she admitted. "But not at you. Not really.

"I called my mother after we talked. She didn't even deny it. She thought she was acting in my best interests, severing ties between us so I would focus on school.

"She was so afraid I would end up like her—alone with a baby, with no education and no job prospects."

"I would have taken care of you, Jess."

She sighed. "That's what my father told my mother. And then, when the reality of a baby was added to the picture, he couldn't get away fast enough."

"That didn't give her the right to interfere."

"No," she agreed. "But it at least explains why she said what she did. And knowing what she told you, knowing you believed it, I can understand why you turned your back on me."

"You can understand," he repeated. "But can you forgive me for believing her?"

"I used to think there wasn't anyone who knew me as well as you did. Now I have to wonder if you ever knew me at all."

"I never meant to hurt you, Jess."

"I never meant to hurt you, either. But it seems we both did a pretty good job of it anyway."

"Do you hate me?"

She shook her head. "I just want to let go of all of the hurt and resentment, to channel my energy in a different direction."

"What does this mean for us? Where do we go from here?"

"It doesn't mean anything except that we've finally discussed our history. Now we need to get over it."

"I've done a lot of thinking about this over the past couple of hours," he said. "And it occurred to me that if we could somehow get around to being friends again, maybe we could work our way toward something more."

She shook her head. "I don't know if we could be friends again. I *do* know that I don't want anything more."

"Why?"

"Because you broke my heart once already and I'm not prepared to give you another chance."

"We're not the same people anymore, Jess."

"No," she agreed. "We haven't been those people for a long time."

"That doesn't mean we can't take some time to know the people we've become."

"I'm only here because of Caleb," she reminded him. "As soon as Caleb is home again, I'll be going back to Manhattan."

She might even be going back sooner, depending on how long Caleb remained in hospital. Steve hadn't been willing to approve her request for a few days' personal leave, so she'd responded by putting in for her two weeks of vacation. And though she refused to consider that Caleb wouldn't be home before that time was up, she knew she might have to return before then. She had obligations at the office that she couldn't continue to ignore.

"I'm not asking you to change your plans for me," Nick said. "Only to let me be part of your life."

It sounded like a simple request, but Jessica knew it wasn't. Because in the few days she'd been back in Pinehurst, she'd realized that she couldn't let him into her life without letting him into her heart. And she absolutely refused to let him into her heart.

Not this time.

Chapter Nine

"Subacute subdural hematoma."

The words spun around in Kristin's head like the buzz of a trapped mosquito.

She shook her head, as if it would make the buzzing stop, as if those words would fade away and the bleeding in her son's brain would miraculously stop.

"What does that mean?" Brian asked.

"It means that there's bleeding inside his skull," the doctor said. "And the bleeding is putting pressure on his brain.

"He needs surgical intervention to decompress the brain, stop any active subdural bleeding and evacuate the hematoma."

"You want to operate on my son's brain?"

"Yes, and we'll need to transfer him to Midtown Children's Hospital in New York City for the surgery."

It wasn't Dr. Marshall this time, but Dr. Reid—the neurologist. The one she'd hoped would finally be able to tell them why Caleb had gone into a coma and, more importantly, when he would wake up again.

She'd still been holding onto hope that it would just happen—that Caleb would open his eyes and everything would be okay. She hadn't anticipated that the doctor would need to operate.

"Is it really necessary?" Brian's voice now, challenging the doctor. "I don't want to put him through any more trauma if we can avoid it."

"It's absolutely necessary, Mr. Clarke." Dr. Reid's response was straightforward and implacable. "The bleeding is exerting pressure inside the skull, pressure that is squeezing your son's brain. If we don't alleviate that pressure, your son will die."

Your son will die.

The buzzing grew louder.

No! She forced her mind to clear, her thoughts to focus. She didn't care what the doctor said—she wasn't going to let Caleb die.

"And what are his chances with the surgery?"

"Stop it!"

Kristin's outburst startled all of them, probably no one more than herself. She'd always deferred to Brian's opinion, always respected his position as head of the household. But this wasn't about what movie to rent on a Saturday night or where to go for summer vacation. This was about their son's life, and it wasn't open for discussion.

She took a deep breath and stared hard at her husband through the tears that filled her eyes. She wanted his support and understanding, but her decision wouldn't be changed regardless. "This is Caleb's life—and if this is his only chance, we have to take it."

She saw her own emotions reflected in his dark eyes: anger, frustration, helplessness, and most of all, fear. She knew it was the fear that made him cautious. Fear of making the wrong decision. Fear that the surgery wouldn't work. Fear that Caleb might die anyway.

But the biggest fear, at least for Kristin, was not doing everything possible to save her son.

Brian nodded, a slight, almost imperceptible, tilt of his head. Relief and gratitude flooded every inch of her, and she reached for his hand, linked their fingers together and squeezed gently.

Then she turned to the doctor. "When can you do the surgery?"

"We're preparing the patient transfer documentation right now. I've called ahead to MCH and booked the OR for eleven o'clock tomorrow morning."

Kristin nodded and the anxiety that had been jumping through her system settled a little. She was still afraid, but they were finally doing something to help Caleb and she believed it was the right thing. She couldn't consider any other possibility.

Nick knew that Kristin wanted Jake and Katie to go to school the day of Caleb's surgery. His sister thought it was important for the kids to stick as closely as possible to their usual routines. But he wasn't surprised when he showed up at the house at barely six o'clock in the morning and found they were waiting with Jessica.

"They didn't want to be anywhere else," Jess explained as they piled into his Explorer. "And I can't imagine they'd be able to concentrate on school while their brother's in surgery."

Nick nodded.

While her explanation was valid, he imagined she was grateful the kids had insisted on coming along. The conversation between him and Jess at the hospital yesterday had left a lot of things still unresolved between them, and Jake and Katie's presence ensured there wouldn't be any more discussion of their relationship.

Jess sniffed the air as she fastened her belt. "Coffee?"

He lifted one of the cups from the holder and passed it to her. Her eyes brightened perceptibly.

"Cream and sugar," he said.

"Bless you." She eased the lid off the cup and sipped carefully.

"Although we're going to be on the road for a few hours, so you could catch some more sleep if you wanted to."

"I can't sleep in the car, it makes me nauseous."

"I can," Katie said from the back, curling up to do just that.

Jake had already settled back in his seat with his Discman and headphones.

"And I can't navigate for you if I'm asleep," Jess continued.

"I'm sure I can find my way to New York City."

She sighed. "Must you always say it like that?"

"Like what?"

"Like it's a four-letter word."

"City is a four-letter word."

"You know what I mean," she chided.

"Okay, I hate New York City. Is that what you wanted me to say?"

She ignored his question to ask, "Why?"

He shrugged. "It's busy and noisy and you were desperate to move there."

"There were opportunities for me in New York that weren't in Pinehurst," she reminded him. "Like Columbia, for example."

"And if you could have gone to college in Pinehurst?" he prompted.

"Okay—I would still have gone to New York. Is that what you wanted me to say?"

No—but it was what he'd expected to hear. What he'd always known.

"It's going to be a long drive," he said again. "Maybe we should talk about something else."

"Maybe we shouldn't even bother trying to make conversation."

"There was a time when we used to be able to talk about anything."

"That's the problem, Nick. That time has passed."

"You really believe that, don't you?"

"It's true."

He shook his head, but he didn't pursue the topic any further. There would be time enough for that later. He intended to make sure of it.

"It was nice of you to give Kristin and Brian the keys to your apartment," Nick said.

"I don't know if they'll actually use it," Jess said. "But at least there's a quiet bed and a private shower if they need to get away from the hospital for a bit."

"Do you live close to MCH?"

"It's about a ten-minute subway ride."

"You ride the subway?"

She smiled. "It's one of the most efficient ways to get

around the city. Cheaper—and often quicker—than the infamous yellow cabs."

"Then why do you own a car?"

"Because the subway lines only go so far and there are times when it's convenient to have independent transportation—despite the fact that I pay a small fortune every month to park my car in a secure lot a few blocks away from my apartment."

"Is that another one of the perks of living in the big city?"

"I love the city," she said, her voice several degrees cooler now. "It's crowded and noisy and busy. And it has the best theaters, museums and shopping."

"And after working eighty hours a week, how much time do you have for the theaters, museums and shopping?"

"Not as much as I would like," she admitted. "But it's nice to know that it's all right there."

"Everything except the moon and the stars."

Her smile was just a little wistful. "The stars are definitely bigger and brighter in Pinehurst."

He waited a beat before venturing to ask, "Have you ever thought of moving back?"

She waited even longer before answering. "Why would I?"

Trust Jess to answer his question with one of her own. Why would she come back when she had everything she apparently wanted in the city? For him? Yeah, that was likely.

Unable to provide a satisfactory response, he remained silent.

Their conversation throughout the rest of the trip was casual and sporadic. At least, until they got into the city. Then Nick was too busy attempting to negotiate through the snarls of downtown traffic to worry about talking.

It was after nine o'clock by the time he pulled into the multilevel parking lot across from the hospital, a good several minutes later before he found a vacant spot, and almost nine-thirty by the time they found Kristin and Brian in the hospital.

By that time, Caleb had already been taken away to be prepped for surgery. So there was nothing left for the six of them to do but wait and worry.

Kristin went down to the chapel to be alone and to bargain with God to save her baby. Once she got there, however, she couldn't pray. She didn't know how to ask God to help Caleb, because she couldn't understand how God could have let such a horrible thing happen to him in the first place.

Her mother used to say that God protects innocents and children. But Caleb was an innocent seven-year-old boy fighting for his life, and Kristin couldn't help thinking that God had failed her little boy. Just as she had.

She was grateful when Jessica came in and sat down beside her, offering a reprieve from these torturous thoughts.

"He's going to pull through this," Jess said.

Kristin so desperately wanted to believe it, but too much had happened over the past few days to let herself maintain any illusions. "It's a risky surgery."

"He's a tough kid—like his mom was." Jess smiled. "Do you remember when you fell out of the apple tree behind my house?"

"I was eleven, and it was a broken collarbone. Caleb—" She swallowed around the tightness of her throat. "He's my baby."

"I know."

But she couldn't know. Not really. Jess didn't have any kids. She didn't know what it was like to rock a fussy baby through the night or suffer with him through the cutting of teeth and the scrapes and bruises that were the badges of childhood. She couldn't understand how every tear her children cried felt as though they'd been wrung out of her own heart.

She didn't know how it felt to sit back, helpless, while her child's life was in the hands of someone else. And she couldn't possibly understand the guilt of knowing that no matter how hard she'd tried, she hadn't been able to protect her baby. No matter how much she'd loved him, it hadn't been enough.

"He was a surprise," Kristin said. "To all of us.

"Jacob was nine, Katie almost eight, when I found out I was pregnant. Brian wasn't thrilled by the news." That was an understatement, and not the complete truth. She forced herself to acknowledge the rest of it.

"Neither was I," she admitted softly. "We were long past the stage of dirty diapers and midnight feedings. It was hard to imagine going back to that again.

"But from the first moment that I held him in my arms—"

She broke off, unable to stifle the sob that tore at her throat.

"Maybe I didn't want him enough. Maybe that's why this is happening."

"No." Jess's voice was firm, unyielding. Then she added, more gently, "It's not your fault. This isn't some kind of divine punishment for any regret you might have had."

More than anything, Kristin wanted to take solace in her friend's conviction. But she couldn't quiet the doubts that continued to plague her.

"All I want is for my life to be the way it was," Kristin admitted. "Even if it wasn't the life I used to dream about."

"I thought this was your dream—to be a wife, a mother."

"So did I. Until I woke up one morning and realized my identity is completely defined by those roles. I've spent eighteen years perfecting an image, becoming the woman I thought I should be. Now I don't know how to be anyone else."

"Why would you want to be anyone else?"

"Because my kids are growing up. Jake's seventeen, more a man than a boy now, and looking forward to college. Kate's almost sixteen and starting to be interested in boys more than school.

"Caleb isn't a baby anymore, either. But at least he still needs me. And I need to be there for him, because he's all I have left."

"Even after the kids are grown up and gone, you'll still have Brian," Jess said soothingly.

"You'd think so," Kristin agreed. "But the truth is, my marriage is falling apart and I don't have the slightest idea how to save it—or even if I want to."

Jess knew she shouldn't be shocked by this revelation. Katie had said her parents were fighting, and Jess had witnessed the tension between them. But this went beyond anything she'd imagined.

"What do you mean, your marriage is falling apart?"

Kristin sighed. "We've been growing apart for a long time. Probably since Caleb was born. Maybe even before that. And now, well…I'm pretty sure Brian's having an affair." A fresh tear slid down her cheek.

She couldn't have been more surprised if Kristin had said that Brian had signed a contract to be the new starting quarterback for the New York Jets. "Why would you think something like that?" she asked cautiously.

"You mean other than the usual reasons?"

"What are the usual reasons?" She realized she should probably know the answer to that question. Then again, though her husband had cheated on her during their marriage, she'd remained blissfully unaware of his infidelity until his mistress had turned up pregnant.

"He's hardly ever home. He'd rather be at football practice or a football game or meetings at the school. Anything to avoid spending time with me. And…we haven't had sex in almost three months."

Jess breathed an inward sigh of relief. "That's hardly conclusive evidence."

Kristin's laugh came out on a sob. "You sound just like a lawyer."

"Guilty."

"But there's something else."

She waited silently.

"This is so hard to admit. I haven't told anyone else— there's no one I could tell. But I can't keep it inside any longer."

"What?"

"There are condoms missing from the box in Brian's dresser. And before you ask, yes, I'm sure.

"Brian had a vasectomy in the spring, but—even though we weren't having sex very often—we continued to use protection until we received confirmation that the procedure was a success. We'd just bought a new box of condoms, used one out of the pack, when we found out we didn't need them anymore.

"A few weeks ago, when I was putting laundry away, I

saw that the condoms had spilled out of the box. I picked them up to put them back and noticed that there were two more missing."

"Have you asked Brian about this?"

"He'd just deny it." Tears filled her eyes. "Or maybe he wouldn't. I don't know which would be worse—to have him lie to me or hear the truth."

"What if there's another explanation?"

Kristin shook her head. "What other explanation could there be? And even if I am wrong about an affair, it won't change the fact that he doesn't love me anymore."

Jessica's heart broke for her friend. "Kris—"

"No, please don't say anything. I just—well, I don't really know why I told you all of this now. Except that I'm so caught up in Caleb I don't have the emotional resources to deal with anything else and I just needed to dump."

"I'm so sorry I haven't been here—for any of this."

Kristin shrugged. "There was nothing you could do."

"I could have listened."

"You did now." She managed a small smile. "I'm really glad you came down here. I thought I wanted to be alone, but when I am, I can't seem to stop the negative thoughts that go through my mind. What if the surgery isn't a success? What if he's already suffered permanent brain damage?" She took a deep breath. "What if he—" her voice faltered, broke "—dies?"

And then her careful composure crumpled and she fell to her knees, sobbing. "Oh God, what if he dies? I couldn't stand it, Jess. I couldn't stand it if I lost my baby."

Jess knelt on the floor beside her friend and wrapped her arms around her trembling shoulders as her own eyes filled with tears. And she sent up a silent and fervent prayer that Kristin wouldn't ever have to know such soul-destroying grief.

Nick was alone in the family waiting room when Jessica returned. He could see the strain on her face, knew this waiting was as difficult for her as it was for the family.

She glanced around the room. "Where are Jake and Katie?"

"I gave them some money and sent them down to the cafeteria for lunch."

She glanced at her watch. "I didn't realize how late it had gotten."

"Are you hungry? We could go join them."

"No, thanks." She pressed a hand to her stomach. "I don't think I could eat anything right now. But you go ahead if you want."

"He's going to be okay."

She forced a smile. "I know."

But he knew that, despite their mutual expressions of confidence, they were both worried.

"How's Kristin holding up?" Nick asked.

"She's strong," Jess reminded him. "So much stronger than anyone should need to be."

"She is. But in spite of my earlier objections, I also know it's helped her to have you here."

"I wanted to stay with her," she admitted. "But Brian came to find her. I think it's important for them to be together and support one another now."

He nodded and took her hand, lacing their fingers together. "I know I didn't make it easy for you to come back to Pinehurst. But I'm glad you did."

"Me, too."

She managed a smile, and he was struck again by how

beautiful she was—even more so now than when she'd been seventeen. Maybe it was the self-confidence she wore like a designer coat, or maybe it was the compassion that softened her golden eyes. Or maybe it was just that she was a woman now instead of a girl, and he was looking at her through the eyes of a man who had never stopped loving her.

The thought, so sudden and unexpected, jolted him.

Was he still in love with Jessica? Or was he only romanticizing their past because of the truth that had finally come to light?

It was difficult not to wonder how differently things might have turned out eighteen years earlier if only they'd talked about the loss of their baby. Or maybe it was naive to think that it would have made a difference—that if he'd known the truth, he and Jessica might still be together. So many things could happen in eighteen years. So many things *had* happened.

He didn't know how long they sat together, holding hands in silence, before Jake and Katie returned. Even then, she didn't draw away from him, so he continued to hold on to her, drawing strength and reassurance from her presence.

Jake sank into one of the seats across from them. "Any news?"

"Not yet."

Katie sat beside her brother, her knees drawn up to her chest, her arms clasped around them. She looked so young and scared. Jake put his arm across her shoulders and she leaned into him a little.

Nick wished there was something he could do to reassure them. Instead, he could only be grateful that they had each other. They were a close family: his sister and her husband, Jacob and Katie and Caleb. They would need that closeness to help them get through this.

The door pushed open again. This time it was Kristin who came through it, with Brian right behind her.

Nick's heart dropped as he saw the tears streaked on his sister's cheeks. Jess, obviously noticing the same thing, gripped his hand tighter as they waited for the news.

It was the most excruciating two seconds of his life before Kristin's lips turned up in a wobbly smile and fresh tears streamed down her cheeks. "The surgery's over and Dr. Reid said everything went well. They got rid of the blood clot and stopped the bleeding."

Katie jumped up. "Caleb's going to be okay?"

Brian laid his hands on Kristin's shoulders, rubbing gently. "The doctor wouldn't make us any promises," he warned, "but he said there's every reason to believe Caleb will fully recover."

Nick's own throat felt tight as he joined in the hugging and laughter, but in the back of his mind he couldn't help wondering what this meant for Jessica. Would she be leaving Pinehurst now, or would she stick around long enough to discover what the future might hold for the two of them together?

After stopping on the road for a quick bite to eat, it was almost seven o'clock when they got home. The light on the answering machine was blinking so Jess checked it right away, wondering if there might be some more news from Kristin already. But both of the messages were for Jake. The first was from Ethan, asking how Caleb's surgery had gone, the second was the manager of DeMarco's Grocery asking if he could come in for a few hours.

Jake decided he could use the extra money and Jess didn't bother to argue. She knew he probably needed the distraction more than the money. So Jake headed off to work and Katie retreated to the living room to finish the homework she hadn't done the night before, leaving Jess and Nick alone again.

"Tired?" Nick asked.

"Exhausted," she admitted. "But I'm too wired to sleep."

"It was a hell of a day, wasn't it?"

"At least the last part was good." She rummaged through the cupboards. "Do you want coffee?"

"I think I've had enough of that today."

"I was thinking decaf," she told him, holding up the tin.

"All right," he said. He opened the cupboard above the stove and pulled out a bottle of Irish whiskey.

"To celebrate?"

"And to help you sleep."

She had no objections on either count and turned the coffeemaker on. It was almost finished dripping through when there was a knock at the back door.

"I'll get it," Nick said, already moving to do so.

"Jake's not home right now," she heard him say. "He went in to work for a few hours."

"I know." She recognized Ethan's voice. "I, uh, came to see Kate."

"Kate?" Nick sounded puzzled.

Jess abandoned the coffee to rescue Ethan. "Kate's in the living room watching *The O.C.* Why don't you go on in?"

"Thanks." Ethan kicked off his shoes inside the door.

"Why is he here to see Katie?" Nick demanded.

Jess only shrugged.

Nick's eyes narrowed. "What do you know that I don't?"

She ducked around him to the fridge. "That good Irish coffee requires whipped cream. Does Kristin have any?"

"No idea," he muttered.

"A-ha." She held up a can of the shake-and-squirt kind. "Perfect."

She poured a generous shot of whiskey into each mug, topped them up with coffee, then swirled whipped cream around the top.

He eyed the frothy topping suspiciously.

"Try it," she said, nudging one of the mugs in his direction.

He picked it up, took a cautious sip. "Not bad."

She took a long swallow, closed her eyes and sighed with pleasure. The coffee was hot and sweet and sinfully indulgent. "Perfect."

"Yeah."

There was something in the throaty response that alerted her. She opened her eyes, saw his gaze fixated on her mouth.

She licked her lips.

"You missed some," he said.

He touched his thumb to the corner of his mouth, wiped away a drop of cream. Then he lifted his thumb to his own mouth, licked it off.

Jess swallowed.

Thankfully, before he could say or do anything else to further weaken her already crumbling defenses, Katie and Ethan came into the kitchen.

"We're going to go for a walk," Katie announced.

With obvious reluctance, Nick tore his gaze from hers to respond to his niece. "Are you finished with your homework?"

She rolled her eyes, already stepping into her shoes. "Yes, I'm finished my homework."

"Even math?"

"Even math."

Nick scowled. "Don't go too far."

"Yes," she said again, obviously just to placate him.

Jess felt her lips twitch but knew better than to let Nick see her smiling. Especially since he was standing at the window, frowning.

"They're holding hands," he said.

She took another sip of her coffee. "So?"

"So she's fifteen."

"Almost sixteen."

His scowl darkened. "They're going down to the creek."

"Relax, Nick." She put her mug down and pulled him away from the window. "They're friends. He knew she'd be worried about Caleb and came by to offer her a distraction."

"I'll bet."

This time she couldn't quite hide the smile. "I don't think it's very different than when you and I were young."

"That's what I'm afraid of."

"Don't you think you're overreacting?"

"I saw the way he was looking at her."

"And if you were paying attention, you'd have seen that she was looking at him the same way."

He sighed, and said again, "She's fifteen."

"I fell in love with you when I was twelve," she admitted softly. "When you threatened to beat up Terry Brennan if he didn't give me back my Scooby Doo lunchbox."

"That's not love, that's infatuation." But he smiled at the memory.

"Maybe," Jess allowed. "The point is, I *thought* I was in love with you."

"Well, Katie's *not* in love with Ethan."

"Did you notice that he's the only one who doesn't call her 'Katie'? He calls her 'Kate.'"

"I get the feeling you're trying to make a point."

"She's growing up, and Ethan's the only one who seems to have noticed."

"He can notice all he wants," Nick said. "As long as he keeps his hands to himself."

"Right. Because teenage boys are the model of self-control," she said dryly.

He started toward the door.

Jess stepped in front of him. "You can't go out there and drag her back here by her hair."

"It's late," he said. "She has school tomorrow."

"You have to trust her, Nick."

He didn't look convinced. "They remind me too much of us."

"Were we ever that young?" she wondered aloud.

"Maybe not that young," he said. "But that completely wrapped up in each other—and look what happened."

Okay, maybe he was right to be concerned.

But even now, even knowing how things had ended between them, how heartbroken she'd been, Jess wouldn't have changed a single thing. Because in the one night she'd spent in Nick's arms, she'd learned what it meant to truly love and be loved.

She sighed a little wistfully, accepting that she would never experience such all-encompassing emotion again. Because she would never risk her heart again.

Chapter Ten

Jessica went through the next morning in a fog. After making sure the kids were up and off to school, she called the hospital only to find out there had been no change in Caleb's condition overnight. Although she shared the disappointment she heard in Kristin's voice, she wasn't really surprised. It had been less than twenty-four hours since he'd undergone major surgery.

After her conversation with Kristin, she sat alone at the kitchen table with her coffee and her thoughts. Unfortunately too many of those thoughts involved Nick—a dangerous direction considering her already melancholy mood.

She thought about trying to busy herself with work, but although Mason was covering the office for a few days it was likely that Nick would be there, too. And she couldn't risk seeing Nick. Not today.

Instead she went down to the creek. She didn't want to

brood, but she couldn't help thinking about everything she and Nick might have had, everything they'd lost. It wasn't usually a path she let her mind wander, but today she didn't seem to be able to stop herself. And here, in the same spot where she and Nick had first made love, she could at least focus on the happier memories.

She'd been so completely and desperately in love with him, willing to do anything and everything for him. The night they'd been together was perfect, magical. Caught up in the moment, neither of them had given a thought to birth control or any other such practical matters. The only thing that had mattered was being together.

Until Jessica had found out she was pregnant. Then their baby had been the only thing that mattered. She'd been so afraid to tell Nick, afraid he'd think she was trying to trap him, afraid he'd accuse her of ruining his life.

He'd been stunned.

Then he'd stunned her by proposing.

She'd been terrified to hope that all of her dreams could be coming true, terrified to let herself believe that he could love her even half as much as she'd loved him. But he'd promised her they would make a life together, that he would never leave her.

And because she'd loved him, she'd believed him.

Then she'd lost their baby, and everything had changed again.

She felt the tears spill onto her cheeks, didn't even try to stop them. In recent years she'd tried to convince herself that it was too far in the past to matter, but only now, finally knowing why Nick had abandoned her, could she let herself mourn.

"I thought I'd find you here."

She hadn't heard Nick approach and averted her head to wipe the tears from her cheeks as he sat down beside her.

"I just needed to be alone, to do some thinking."

He traced the trail of moisture down her cheek. "Since when does thinking involve tears?"

"It's been an emotional few days," she said. "I guess everything just caught up with me."

He nodded but didn't speak.

"What are *you* doing here, Nick?"

"Looking for you."

"Why?"

"Because today is September twenty-second."

She hadn't expected him to remember a date she'd thrown at him in the heat of an argument. Hadn't expected it would matter. The fact that it did warmed something deep inside her.

"Yes, it is," she said softly.

He slipped an arm across her shoulders, pulled her closer.

"You're going to make me cry again."

"I'm a tough guy. I can handle it."

"I don't do this every year," she said, sniffling against his shoulder. "But this year…I don't know why it's affecting me like this."

"Emotional overload. Because of Caleb. Because of everything that's happened between us."

"Yeah." She sniffled again.

He lifted her gently and settled her onto his lap. "Let me hold you, Jess. Let me be here for you, as I should have been there for you when we lost our baby."

His quiet understanding completely undid her. He

rocked her gently as she cried, offering only silent unwavering support. And cry she did. She cried until his shirt was soaked through, until there weren't any tears left inside.

Still Nick held her, cradling her against the solid warmth of his chest, his hand stroking over her hair.

After what seemed like an eternity, she managed to find her voice. "I'm sorry. I came back to support Kristin and Brian, and I'm the one falling apart."

"I'd say you're entitled."

She tipped her head back to meet his gaze, not caring that her eyes were puffy and swollen, her nose red. She needed to see him, and she needed him to see that she meant what she was saying. "I wanted our baby, Nick."

He tightened his arms around her. "I know you did."

Then he kissed her.

His lips were warm and gentle, coaxing rather than demanding. His tongue traced the shape of her mouth, then dipped inside, teasing, tempting. She felt herself yielding, responding. Not giving in, but giving everything.

It had never been any other way with Nick. And it was exactly why she'd balked when he'd asked her to let him be part of her life. Because being with Nick meant loving Nick, and she wasn't prepared to risk that again.

This time it was she who pulled away, leaning her head back against his shoulder.

"Was that a kiss to make it better?" she asked, keeping the question light, casual.

"That was a kiss because I needed to kiss you."

"I thought you wanted to be friends."

"Yeah, I thought that was what I wanted, too. At least to start."

He skimmed a fingertip over the curve of her bottom lip,

tempting her to kiss him again, to lose herself in the way she felt when she was in his arms. But there was too much history tangled up in the passion, too many emotions entwined with the needs.

It would be so easy to fall in love with him again. Easy and crazy. Because no matter what might happen between them, she would be going back to Manhattan soon. Her life was there; his was here.

"I can give you friendship," she said. "But I can't give you anything more than that."

"Can't or won't?"

"Can't," she whispered, her heart pleading with him to understand.

He pressed his lips to the top of her head. "Then we'll start with friendship."

Brian was worried about Kristin.

She'd been holding up so well through this whole ordeal with Caleb. Maybe too well. He didn't know how much longer she could hold everything together without falling apart.

Or maybe he wasn't giving her enough credit. Kristin was a truly incredible woman—steady and strong. So much stronger than he was.

He wished he could ease some of her burden, but she didn't seem to want or need his help. She didn't seem to want anything from him anymore.

When had everything gone so wrong between them? When had they stopped sharing their lives and started to merely coexist?

He had no idea. He only knew that he missed the way things used to be. He missed the woman she used to be.

He wanted to see her smile, hear her laugh. It had been too long since he'd heard her laugh.

He shifted his chair closer to Caleb's bed.

Kristin had asked him to sit with their son while she went to grab a quick shower. As much as he hated being in this sterile room, seeing Caleb like this, he couldn't refuse when she asked him for so little.

He tugged the sheet up a little higher, as if he was just tucking him into bed for the night, and tried not to stare at the tubes and monitors that were attached to various parts of his body. He ignored the hiss and beep and hum of the machines and reached out to hold his son's small hand.

He remembered when Jake was a baby—so tiny and fragile and perfect. Now, Jake's hands were almost as big as his own. Then there was Katie—even smaller and somehow more delicate, but she'd wrapped his heart around her littlest finger from the beginning. And years later, Caleb had come into their lives. He was their baby—their last tie, their last chance.

His eyes burned, his throat ached.

"We need you, Caleb." It was a whispered plea, a heartfelt prayer. "Your mom and I, we need you to pull through this." He choked on a sob, felt the splash of hot tears on his cheeks. "Because if you don't, I don't know that we will, either."

He wiped the back of his hand over his face and thought about everything he and Kristin had been through over the years, all that they'd endured together.

Lately she'd been pulling away from him, withdrawing into herself. And he didn't know how to reach her. He still loved her, but he was starting to wonder if love was enough anymore.

He felt a flutter and his heart skipped.

He stared down at his son's hand tucked inside his own.

Had he imagined it? Or had Caleb's fingers moved?

He held his breath, waiting.

Exhaled slowly, disappointment sinking like a lead weight into the pit of his belly.

"We could really use a miracle about now," he said.

He didn't know if he was talking to Caleb or some higher power. He only wished that someone would answer.

The alarm on one of the monitors sounded.

Brian's heart skipped. He dropped Caleb's hand and ran for the door, noticed the nurse was already on her way. He hadn't even called for her and she was there. "What happened? What's wrong?"

She pressed a few buttons, silencing the alarm.

Then she smiled at him. "Nothing's wrong, Mr. Clarke. This machine is an SMIV—a synchronized mechanical intermittent ventilator. It's programmed to insure that Caleb receives a specified number of breaths and the right volume of oxygen every minute."

"But why did it go off?"

Her smile widened. "To let us know that he's starting to breathe on his own."

His heart filled with hope, expanding inside his chest.

"Now I'm going to check for a withdrawal response." She pressed into his fingernail bed. Caleb's hand jerked away. "I'll go get the doctor."

He wanted to go get Kristin, but he didn't dare walk away for a second. Not now.

Maybe it was coincidence, maybe it was intuition, but suddenly she was there. "What's going on?"

He picked up their son's hand again. He was afraid to

say it, afraid it might not be true. But Caleb's fingers twitched again and gave him hope. He had to share that hope with Kristin. "I think he might be waking up."

He saw the tears shimmering in her eyes, knew that she was waging the same internal battle between hope and fear.

"Come here," he said gently.

She moved closer.

He reached for her hand and placed it on top of Caleb's, so that their son's palm was clasped between both of theirs.

Her eyes widened. "He moved."

Brian nodded.

She shifted her hand, linking her fingers with his, using her thumb to trace circles over the back of Caleb's palm. "Hey, baby. Mommy and Daddy are here with you."

He heard the door push open, footsteps, but he didn't tear his gaze away from his son.

"What's the excitement in here?" Dr. Reid asked.

"We think Caleb's starting to wake up."

There was a soft, hoarse whimper.

"He opened his eyes." Kristin squeezed Brian's fingers. "Did you see that? He opened his eyes."

"He did," Dr. Reid agreed.

There was another slow blink, then his eyes closed again. But this time, instead of a whimper, he said, "Mom."

"Ohmygod." Kristin closed her eyes, tears spilling freely onto her cheeks. "He's waking up. He's really waking up."

Brian didn't respond. He couldn't say anything around the lump in this throat.

But Kristin started to laugh. She was laughing and crying at the same time and then, in the midst of it all, she kissed him.

* * *

Jess smiled at the offering Nick placed in front of her—a steaming bowl of tomato soup and a perfectly toasted grilled cheese sandwich.

He took a seat across from her. "Are you mocking my culinary effort? I know it's not gourmet fare, but—"

"No," she interrupted. "I was just thinking that no one—other than my mother and yours—have ever cooked for me before."

"It's soup and a sandwich—I'm not sure that really counts as cooking."

"It's perfect comfort food," she insisted. "Thank you."

"If you're impressed by this, you should see what I can do with a steak and a grill."

She smiled again. "Yes, I can see how that would be more your style. Man—meat—fire."

He grinned and dipped his spoon into the soup. "When you say no one has ever cooked for you, does that include your ex?" There was no censure in his tone, just curiosity.

"We were a modern professional couple with equally demanding jobs, so we had an established arrangement for meals. On Sundays, Tuesdays and Thursdays, I cooked. On Mondays, Wednesdays and Fridays, Steve picked something up for dinner. On Saturdays, we went out."

"He picked up dinner three times a week?"

"Well, sometimes he had it delivered." She nibbled on a corner of her sandwich. "Or we'd go out to eat. One of the greatest things about Manhattan is the variety of restaurants—Italian, Indian, Greek, Chinese, Japanese, Vietnamese. Anything you could think of."

"I bet there isn't a Mama Leone's."

Jess sighed. "It wasn't a comparison, Nick."

He stacked his dishes, carried them to the dishwasher. "Sorry. It was a knee-jerk reaction."

Because he'd gone out of his way to be nice to her, she decided to let it pass. "Thank you for coming to find me down by the creek."

"Are you talking about today—or that night so many years ago?"

"Today." But she smiled, because she knew that his question was only intended to lighten the mood.

"Just wondering."

"Getting back to my point," she continued.

"You don't have to thank me, Jess. I was glad to be with you."

This time her smile came more easily. "I almost forgot what a nice guy you could be."

He winced. "The greatest insult to a man's ego—being described by a woman as 'nice.'"

"How is that an insult?"

"Because what it really means is that the man referred to has absolutely no hope of ever seeing that woman naked."

She couldn't help but laugh. "Do you really believe that?"

He nodded solemnly. "It's like when a guy describes a woman as having a great personality, what it really means is that she's unattractive."

"I've been told that I have a great personality."

"You do," he agreed. "But it's not the first thing that would come to a guy's mind if he was asked to describe you."

"What would come to mind?" she asked warily.

He grinned. "Hot."

She laughed. "Now I know you're joking."

"I'm not. That's exactly the word Mason used to describe you the other day."

"Ah. Mason." She nodded. "Didn't we agree that Mason was easily impressed?"

"Yes, but he does have impeccable taste."

"How did we get off on this tangent?" she wondered aloud.

"You said I was 'nice,'" he reminded her, obviously still insulted.

"Because you are." She reached across the table to take his hand.

He grew serious. "I'm glad we finally talked about what happened. But I can't help wishing we'd had the conversation a long time ago."

She shrugged. "I don't know that anything would have been different."

"*Everything* would have been different. Everything *can* be different, Jess."

She shook her head. "Eighteen years have gone by. We can't undo that with one heart-to-heart conversation."

"I don't want to undo it. I want to move forward."

He was breaking her heart, promising something she wanted more than anything, something she knew they couldn't have.

"We owe it to ourselves to try, Jess."

"If this is because you're feeling guilty—"

"I'm feeling a lot of things," he interrupted. "Maybe guilt is one of them. But it's not the reason."

"Then…why?"

"Because we never had the chance to be together."

"Maybe things would have been different if we'd each known the truth years ago. But the fact is, we don't know each other at all anymore."

"We can get to know one another again."

She shook her head. "It won't change anything."

"How can you be sure?"

"Even if we found there was still some kind of connection—"

"There's definitely a—" he paused meaningfully "—connection."

She didn't know whether to be amused or exasperated. "You're talking about sexual attraction, and that's all you've focused on since I got here."

He frowned. "You're so wrong."

"The point I'm trying to make," she continued, "is that whatever attraction may exist, there's no rational reason to pursue it."

"Does everything always have to be rational?"

"Yes." Her response was firm, unapologetic.

"You never do anything without a plan or purpose?"

"No." Except for the kisses she'd shared with Nick, but she wasn't about to acknowledge that.

He lifted an eyebrow, no doubt remembering those same kisses.

"Not anymore."

"Hmm." He lowered his head and traced his lips over her jaw, nibbled his way down her neck.

She managed to resist the impulse to sigh at the pleasure of his touch. Instead, she took a careful step back. "I told you when we were at the creek that I can't offer you anything more than friendship."

"Yet you're too honest to deny the attraction between us."

"I'm not denying anything," she said. "I'm only telling you what can and cannot happen."

"When was the last time you let yourself do something spontaneous?"

His question forced her to remember exactly why she

tried so hard not to give in to her impulses. "The night of Kristin and Brian's wedding."

"The night we made love in the moonlight."

She could only nod.

"Was that really such a bad thing?"

"Only because we didn't think about the potential consequences."

"This time we will."

"No."

"Stop being so negative. If you won't let yourself be impulsive, we'll have to establish a plan and purpose for becoming reacquainted."

"There is no plan or purpose."

"Come on," he said. "I'm trying to play by your rules. The least you could do is play along."

She sighed but refrained from further comment.

"Part one of the plan is to spend time together."

"I've already been spending time with you."

He shook his head. "I'm talking about time away from the hospital and my office and my sister's house."

Still she hesitated. "Okay."

Nick grinned. "Part two is to get you back into my bed."

She couldn't claim to be overly surprised by this information, although she was surprised that he'd expressed it so directly. "That's creative," she said dryly.

The curve of his lips was slow, seductive. "It could be."

She swallowed. "And the purpose?"

"Pleasure." He skimmed his fingertip down her throat, then over the buttons on the front of her shirt. "Mutual pleasure."

"I'm, uh, not sure…" Her words trailed off as his lips began to follow the path he'd just traced.

"What…are you…not…sure…about?" the words were interspersed between teasing brushes of his mouth against her skin.

"This."

Oh, how she wanted him.

"You. Me."

Definitely wanted him.

"Us."

Desperately wanted him.

"Everything."

But wanting him wasn't enough. She made herself draw back.

"If you're not sure, we'll take it slow." He nibbled his way up to her ear, along her jaw. "Until you are."

She would be crazy to succumb to his erotic assault on her senses.

The shrill ring of the telephone was a welcome interruption. Except that Nick made no move to answer it. Instead he slid his hands up her back, drawing her closer to the solid heat of his body.

"Don't you think you should get that?"

"I'd rather kiss you."

And in that moment, she wanted nothing more than to be kissed by him, to kiss him back.

The phone rang again, breaking the seductive web he was weaving around her.

"It might be Kristin."

The possibility banked some of the fire in his eyes.

"You're right." He stepped toward the phone, but hesitated before picking it up. "We'll get back to this."

It was a promise that made her tingle with equal parts apprehension and anticipation.

Chapter Eleven

Nick and Jessica went to the high school to share the news about Caleb waking up with Jake and Katie.

"We should do something to celebrate," Nick said.

"I was thinking we could have a 'welcome home' party," Jess said. "Once Caleb is released from the hospital."

"I feel like we should do something now, even though Caleb isn't here," Katie said. "I know. Let's go for ice cream."

"Good idea." Nick grinned at Jess. "It's a family tradition—celebrating important occasions with ice cream."

So they all piled into his SUV and drove over to Walton's Ice Cream Parlor.

Jess climbed out of the passenger side, hesitated. "Isn't this the same place we used to come to when we were kids?"

"Yes, it is."

Jake and Katie were already walking through the door,

but Nick didn't try to hurry Jessica. He knew from experience it would take Katie a while to decide what she wanted. Jake would have a hot fudge sundae with nuts, and Jessica would likely order strawberry.

It was strange that after so much time had passed, he still remembered the little things like her favorite flavor of ice cream. And the bigger things, like the way she trembled when his kissed her neck, and—

He shook off the memories, knowing he was only torturing himself. Jess had made it clear that she had no intention of being easily seduced. So he would go slow, give her time to get used to the idea.

He wasn't worried. He believed that anything worth having was worth waiting for. And Jess was definitely worth having.

She frowned, and for a moment he wondered if he'd spoken that last thought aloud. He exhaled a silent breath when he realized she was still staring at the sign over the door.

"Did they tear the old building down?" she asked.

"Nope—just renovated it."

"It had to be a pretty major renovation."

"It was," he agreed. "Mason and I did the design."

"Really?"

He nodded.

"It's fabulous."

It wasn't anything he hadn't heard before. The Walton redesign had been one of their first—and still one of their most famous—projects. But it meant a lot to him that Jessica could see and appreciate his work.

"Thanks," he said. "But the best thing about this place is still the ice cream."

"Is it still homemade?"

"You bet."

"My mouth is watering already."

As he suspected, Katie was still pondering her options when they got inside. Jake went ahead and ordered a hot fudge sundae with nuts, Jess went for a double-scoop strawberry cone, Nick opted for a double-scoop of chocolate chip, and Katie finally decided on a double chocolate brownie sundae.

He and Jess were halfway through their cones when a group of kids from the high school walked in. Jake, being a growing teenage boy, had already finished his and immediately excused himself to go say "hi" to some friends.

Nick recognized Ethan and a couple other guys from the football team, but it was the girls who had come in with them that seemed to have Jake's attention. Or one girl in particular.

"I'm guessing that's Lara," Jess said, following his gaze.

"Good guess." He noticed that one of the other girls was sticking pretty close to Ethan, and he breathed a silent sigh of relief. Whatever vibes he'd thought he sensed passing between his niece and her brother's best friend had obviously just been a product of his imagination. He glanced at his nephew again, at the smitten look on his face. "And I'm guessing that Jake is definitely over Becky."

"A teenage boy's heart is fickle," Jess said.

"Not always," Nick denied.

She shrugged, but her attention was focused on Katie, not him. "Did you want to go?"

Nick frowned at the half-eaten sundae in front of his niece. "She's not finished with her ice cream."

Katie squared her shoulders and picked up her spoon.

Jess frowned but resumed nibbling around the edge of

her cone, leaving Nick with the distinct impression that he was missing out on something.

Then Ethan wandered away from the group and approached their table. "I heard the good news about Caleb," he said. "Does this mean he'll be coming home soon?"

"We don't know yet," Nick said. "But hopefully it won't be too long."

"Maybe we can arrange a rematch of our basketball game before you go back," he said, speaking to Jessica this time.

The question jolted Nick back to reality. Somehow, in the space of only a few days, he'd started taking Jessica's presence for granted. But she was only in Pinehurst temporarily and soon she would be going back to her life in New York City. The realization depressed him.

"Maybe," Jess finally said to Ethan, her response decidedly noncommittal.

Before Nick had a chance to wonder about it, Jake came over to join them. With him was a girl he introduced as Lara, and Nick noticed that the top of his nephew's ears turned pink as he made the introductions.

Jake slid into the booth beside Jess, gesturing for Lara to join him.

"Have a seat," Jake said to Ethan.

Ethan glanced warily at Katie before sliding onto the bench beside her.

They chatted for a few minutes, until Lara said she had to go and Jake jumped up to offer to walk her home. Then Katie started to complain that she had a ton of homework she needed to start on, so Ethan said he'd walk her to the library—which got Nick wondering about those vibes all over again—but he didn't object. The departure of all the kids meant he and Jess were finally going to be alone again.

And then his ex-wife walked in.

* * *

Jess saw them first. A man with a square jaw, a military-style haircut, and warm brown eyes. But it was the woman who caught her attention, not just because she was gorgeous, but because there was something vaguely familiar about her. The man's arm was around her shoulders, and as she tipped her head back to laugh at something he said, he pressed a quick kiss to her mouth.

She felt an uncomfortable pang of envy at the display of easy affection and obvious happiness, but she kept watching them, anyway. They joined the line at the counter, still cuddled close together, and the man splayed his hand over the gentle swell of her belly.

The pang cut sharper and deeper this time. Not envy but emptiness. She swallowed hard and averted her gaze quickly. So she wasn't prepared for the woman to show up at the table where she sat with Nick.

"Hello, Nick." Her voice was soft, melodious.

He nodded tersely. "Tina."

Now Jessica knew why the woman looked familiar— the first time they'd met, the last time she'd seen her, Tina had been married to Nick.

"I heard about Caleb," she said, her soft blue eyes reflecting genuine concern and compassion. "Is he okay?"

"He's going to be," Nick told her. "We got a call from Kristin today."

Tina nodded. "That's great news. I wanted to stop by the hospital when I first heard about the accident, but I wasn't sure if Kristin would be glad to see me."

"She would have," he said. "I'll tell her you were asking about Caleb."

"Okay." Still she hesitated, glancing from Nick to Jessica to her husband in line at the counter and back to Nick again.

Jess took the hint. "I'll...um...just go wash up."

Tina sent her a quick smile and slid into the newly vacated seat.

Jess took her time lathering her hands with soap and tried not to think about Nick and Tina. She glanced up at the mirror, and nearly cringed at the reflection staring back at her. There were tiny lines around her eyes and dark shadows beneath them. And although she'd put on a touch of eyeliner and lipstick in the morning, after her crying jag at the creek, there was no trace of either.

Not that it mattered. No amount of cosmetics could make her ten years younger or turn her into a gorgeous blue-eyed blonde. It made her wonder how Nick could possibly be attracted to her when he'd once been married to a woman who looked as though she could be a cover model.

"Jessica?"

She saw Tina approaching, forced a smile as she turned off the faucet.

"I wanted to thank you for giving me a minute alone with Nick."

"No problem." She reached for a paper towel.

"I think he was blindsided by my pregnancy, and I just wanted to smooth over any awkwardness."

"You don't have to explain anything to me."

Tina hesitated a moment before asking, "Did he ever tell you why he and I split up?"

"Before this week, I hadn't seen Nick in years," she said, just to set the record straight. "And whatever happened between the two of you is none of my business."

Unfortunately, Tina didn't take the hint. "Nick wanted kids from the start. We'd barely said our 'I dos' and he was talking about a family. I was the one who wanted to wait.

"It wasn't that I didn't want to have a baby—obviously." She rubbed a hand over her slightly rounded tummy and smiled. "But that I didn't want to have a baby with a man who was more committed to the idea of a family than he was to me."

"He married you." Jess didn't know why she felt compelled to point out the fact in Nick's defense, but did so anyway.

Tina nodded. "But he didn't love me. Oh, he told me he did, and I think he even believed it. But after three years of trying to make him love me the way I needed to be loved, I finally realized he never would—because I wasn't you."

Jess was certain there wasn't anything she could say or do to alleviate the awkwardness of the moment, so she remained silent.

"He never told me about you," Tina continued. "Not until I met you at his mom's funeral, and even then I had to ask some very pointed questions. Then again, I didn't need to hear his answers. Because the moment I saw him look at you, I knew that he would never be able to look at me or any other woman the same way."

"Nick and I had a past," Jess admitted. "But even six years ago, it was a distant past."

"Maybe distant, but not forgotten. I'm not telling you this to make you uncomfortable," Tina said. "And I certainly don't blame you for the breakup of my marriage. I'm telling you because it was seeing the way Nick looked at you that made me realize I wanted the same thing, that I wouldn't be happy settling for anything less.

"I am happy now," she added softly. "And I want Nick to be happy, too."

"I don't think his happiness is dependent upon me," Jess said.

Tina frowned. "Maybe not entirely. But he needs someone to help him find balance in his life, someone to make him realize his career isn't everything."

Jess wanted to disregard what Tina had said. But even after she'd gone and Nick had taken her back to Kristin and Brian's house, she couldn't forget her words. Or the irony of her thinking that Jess could help Nick find some balance in his life when Jess had none in her own. Her career *was* everything to her. Or it had been, until one phone call had brought her back to Pinehurst and made her question every aspect of her life.

But being back here, away from her work, had reassured her about her career choice. Because she did love her job. Sometimes it was frustrating and demanding, but it was also challenging and rewarding.

Being here had also made her realize, even before her conversation with Tina, that she needed to find a way to round out her life. She needed to take the time to do the things she loved—walk in the park, go to the theater, play basketball. She needed to make time for herself—to meet people who weren't associates or clients or otherwise connected with Dawson, Murray & Neale.

She'd also realized that she'd never been truly happy after her breakup with Nick. She'd been so hurt by his abandonment, she hadn't been able to completely open up to anyone else—including her husband. She'd married Steve, but she'd never told him about her past with Nick or the baby they'd lost because she'd refused to let herself be so vulnerable again.

Nick knew her better than anyone else ever had, but there was still something he didn't know. Something she couldn't bring herself to tell him because she wasn't strong enough to open herself up to rejection again.

She sighed. Life was a series of choices and she'd made hers. If she could live her life over again, maybe she would have done some things differently, but ultimately, she'd done what she needed to do.

Now, as much as she wanted to be with Nick, it simply wasn't possible for them to have a future together. Then again, he hadn't said anything to her about a future. His only goal was to get her into bed. He knew she was going back to the city in a couple of weeks. So obviously whatever plans he had for the two of them didn't extend beyond that time period.

If that was the case, why couldn't she give him what he wanted? What, truthfully, they both wanted?

She knew it would be difficult, if not impossible, to share her body with him and not open her heart. She also knew it was already too late to keep an emotional distance.

She'd shared so much with him over the past few days, there was no way she could expect to go back to New York unscathed. How could it hurt any more to enter into a physical relationship? As long as she kept it simple and honest, knowing it was only for now and not forever, what was the harm?

Nick was debating the merits of frozen lasagna versus Chinese takeout when he heard the doorbell. He closed the door of the freezer and glanced at the clock on the microwave. Eight forty-two. It was a little late for a big meal anyway, he decided as he made his way toward the front of the house. Maybe he'd settle for a bag of microwaved popcorn while he watched the game.

He pulled open the door and found Jessica on the porch.

Jessica in navy tailored slacks that hugged her hips and a silky blouse in a lighter color with at least three buttons undone. From a height advantage of several inches, he could see more than just a hint of cleavage and no evidence of a bra.

His mouth went dry as it occurred to him that he'd much prefer her to either frozen lasagna or Chinese. But why had she come? Didn't she know how her nearness affected him? How he'd be tempted to kiss her again and feel tortured when she withdrew?

Then she smiled and he noted the sparkle in her eye and the bottle of champagne in her hand, and he thought maybe he could guess why she'd come—if not the reason for her change of heart.

"It's not ice cream," she said, holding up the bottle for his inspection. "But I thought it might be appropriate for a more personal celebration. Can I come in?"

He could imagine licking champagne off her naked body, and he stepped back quickly to allow her entry. "I thought you weren't sure about this. Us."

"I changed my mind." She put the bottle of champagne down and moved toward him, sliding her palms up his chest, over his shoulders. "I'm hoping you haven't?"

His mind went blank. "Haven't what?"

"Changed your mind." She pressed her lips to his throat, nipped at his earlobe.

"About…what?"

She traced the curve of his bottom lip with her tongue. "Wanting me in your bed."

Then she kissed him, a full-out sensual assault of lips and tongue that nearly had him groaning.

"Do you?" She whispered the question against his lips. "Do you still want me, Nick?"

"Yes." *Definitely yes.* In capital letters and flashing lights.

His hands slid up her torso, drawing her close, closer.

He found the buttons at the front of her shirt, made quick work of unfastening them. She shivered as his hands slid over her naked flesh, skimming the sides of her breasts.

Definitely no bra.

"Damn, you're killing me here, Jess."

His thumbs brushed over the already tight peaks. She responded by pressing her body closer, wriggling against him. He pushed the blouse over her shoulders, down her arms, pinning them behind her back. Then he dipped his head and fastened his mouth over one peaked nipple.

Jessica gasped, then shifted to press her hips against his, rocking against the hard length of his erection. His eyes nearly rolled back in his head.

Instead, he shifted to a safer distance and tugged her shirt back into place. "We're not going to do this."

She blinked, her eyes going from dazed to stunned in half a second. "I thought this was what you wanted."

"Not like this."

She turned away and began refastening her buttons. "I thought you wanted me to be impulsive."

"And I thought you wanted to be practical."

"That was before you got me all hot and bothered."

He couldn't help but smile. "Hot and bothered, huh?"

She glared at him.

"You know it's not that I don't want you, Jess. It's that I don't want to rush into something we're not ready for."

"It seemed to me that we were both more than ready." She tucked her blouse into her slacks.

"I'm more ready than you could possibly imagine." The painful tightness in his jeans was proof of that fact. "But I'm not convinced you are."

"I'm not seventeen anymore, Nick."

"No, you're not," he agreed. "But it's still September twenty-second and I don't want to take advantage of you when I know how vulnerable you're feeling."

"It'll be the twenty-third in a few more hours."

How many times did a man have to try to do the right thing before he could be forgiven for succumbing to his own needs? But as much as he wanted to take what Jess was offering, he knew it wasn't really what either of them wanted. She wanted to lose herself in the mindless pleasure of sex, and he wanted…

He wasn't quite sure what he wanted, except that he wanted more.

So instead of licking champagne off of her naked body, he turned her fully clothed one back toward the door. "Tomorrow night," he said. "I'll pick you up at seven."

"For what?"

"Dinner."

She laughed. "Do you have some misguided notion that it's more gentlemanly to buy a woman dinner before you take off her clothes?"

"Not necessarily," he denied. "Although it did occur to me that while I've had the distinct pleasure of taking off your clothes before, I've never bought you dinner."

"We could order pizza."

The woman could tempt a saint. And he knew he wasn't anywhere near to being a saint. But he was determined to resist—to prove to himself that he could, and to show Jessica that sex wasn't all he wanted from her.

"I think we can do better than pizza."

Then he kissed her again, tucking his hands inside his pockets to make sure they stayed off her this time.

"Seven o'clock," he said again.

"I'll be waiting." She paused at the door and glanced over her shoulder. "Unless I get a better offer."

Chapter Twelve

He'd turned her down.

She'd offered him sex, simple and straightforward, and he'd sent her home.

Jess didn't feel rejected so much as baffled by the turn of events. He was the one who'd said he wanted her back in his bed. Then, when she decided she wouldn't mind being there, he had a sudden change of heart. Or was he just playing hard to get?

It was a question she couldn't help but ponder through the night, alone in her bed, and throughout the next morning in Nick's office.

If he was determined to resist her, as his behaviour both last night and this morning indicated, she had only one option: to make herself irresistible.

So she left the office promptly at one and went shopping. She'd been wandering down Main Street thinking she might buy something new for her date with Nick but not really expecting to find anything appropriate. And then she saw it, in the front window of a little boutique, and she knew she had to have it.

It was black crepe, sleeveless, with a V-neck front and back, and a skirt that ended just below her knees. Simple, elegant and sexy.

Then, of course, she needed the proper lingerie to go with it. And new shoes. By the end of the day, when she got back to Kristin and Brian's with an armload of shopping bags, she was feeling much better about the evening ahead.

When Nick picked her up and she had the pleasure of watching his tongue almost fall out of his mouth, she knew the dress was worth every penny.

"You…um…wow."

It wasn't a very eloquent compliment, but it was certainly a satisfying one.

He took her to Le Coeur for dinner, a new upscale Mediterranean restaurant. She took a moment to look around as they waited for the maitre d'. The walls were covered with textured silk, the floors with thick burgundy carpet. The light from the chandeliers was muted, the music piped from hidden speakers was soft. And the delicious aromas of spices and sauces that lingered in the air made her mouth water.

They were led to the second floor, through the upstairs dining room, and out to a private table on the balcony. It was a beautiful fall night and the stone terrace had a wonderful view of the gardens below.

The maitre d' pulled out her chair and placed her napkin across her lap. Then their server came by to introduce himself and deliver the menus, followed by the sommelier with the wine list.

"This is…incredible," she said to Nick.

"Worth waiting for?" he asked.

She smiled. "We haven't eaten yet."

"Why don't we start with some wine?"

"Sounds good."

So he ordered a bottle of pinot noir and an antipasto appetizer for them to share. For dinner Jess had the fettuccine with hot Italian sausage and wild mushrooms in a vodka cream sauce; Nick had the grilled chicken brochettes with a tomato basil tapenade. Of course, she had to try a bite of his and he had a taste of hers. Then, even though she was sure she couldn't eat anything else, he ordered a pineapple and champagne sorbet for dessert and she couldn't resist a little sample.

Throughout the meal, their conversation flowed as easily as the wine. They shared old memories and talked about new dreams. It was easy and fun and made Jess remember exactly what she'd lost when she'd lost Nick.

Nick's thoughts must have paralleled her own because he finally asked, "What really went wrong between us, Jess?"

Attempting to keep the conversation light, she responded, "I'm guessing it was the whole unplanned pregnancy thing."

He smiled wryly. "I never thought that was such a terrible occurrence."

"Didn't you?" She shook her head. "You actually offered to marry me."

"And that panicked you," he guessed.

"I was seventeen years old. Everything about sex and love and marriage and babies panicked me."

"I wanted to marry you."

She picked up her glass of wine, noted that he'd refilled it again. "You wanted to do the right thing."

"Only because doing the right thing would have got me what I wanted."

Jessica sighed. "I'm so sorry about the baby, Nick."

"I wasn't talking about the baby, Jess. I was talking about you."

"Oh." She didn't know what else to say and was grateful that their conversation was interrupted by the waiter delivering the check.

Nick settled up the bill and pushed back his chair. "What do you want to do now?" he asked her.

She glanced at her watch, surprised to see that it was almost eleven o'clock. "I should probably be getting back."

"Are you going to turn into a pumpkin at midnight?"

"No, but your carriage might."

"I'll take my chances." He offered her his hand. "Let's go for a walk."

"Walk?" She fell into step beside him.

"It's a primitive method of transportation—simple yet effective." He led her outside, turned toward the park. "See? You're catching on already."

"I know what it is," she said. "I just don't know why you want to walk or where you want to go."

"I want to walk so that I can spend some more time with you, and I want to walk somewhere dark so I can kiss you."

"Oh."

He ducked under a tree and turned to face her, grinning. "That honesty stuff kind of throws you, doesn't it?"

"A little," she admitted.

"Would you have preferred if I'd said I just wanted to look at the moon and the stars?"

"Only if it's true."

"The truth is that I love the way the moonlight shines on your hair—" he stroked a hand over her hair, tugged on the ends to tip her head back "—the way the stars reflect in your eyes."

"That has to be one of the cheesiest pickup lines I've ever heard," she said, laughing.

His smile was easy. "It was cheesy, wasn't it?"

She nodded.

"It was also the truth."

And somehow, her heart melted just a little. "Is this the part where you're going to kiss me?"

"I was getting to that," he said.

And then, finally, his lips brushed over hers. Softly. Gently. Fleetingly.

He started to draw away.

"More." She put her arms around his neck and dragged his mouth down to hers.

"Okay," he said, several minutes later. "I think maybe now it's time to get you home before I forget that I've decided to take things slow this time."

"It's not the twenty-second anymore," she reminded him.

"I've been aware of that since twelve-oh-one this morning. But we both need time to think about this and be sure it's what we want."

"We don't have a lot of time," she said. "I have to go back to the city at the end of next week."

"Which means we have nine whole days between now and then to figure this out."

"Nick—"

He cut off her protest with a quick kiss.

"Nine days is more than we've ever had together before."

He kissed her again, longer, lingering this time.

"Please."

She leaned her forehead against his chest. "I can't give you any more than those nine days."

"Then that will have to be enough. For now."

When Jess walked around to the back door after Nick dropped her off, she found Katie on the porch.

"Can't sleep?" she asked, sitting down beside her.

Katie shook her head.

"Any particular reason?"

"I hate my life."

Jess smiled. "I used to say that when I was your age, too."

"At least you got out of this town," Katie said. "If it's up to my dad and Uncle Nick and Jake, I'll be stuck here forever."

"It's not up to anyone but you, Katie. After graduation, you can go wherever you want to go."

"Graduation's a long time away," she muttered.

Jess smiled again. "I know it seems that way. But in the meantime, you have choices to make, decisions about what you want that will take you where you want to go."

"I'm trying to make my own decisions," Katie said. "But no one trusts that I'm old enough to know what I want."

"Does 'no one' refer to anyone in particular?"

Katie huffed out a breath. "Ethan."

Jess stayed silent, waiting for her to explain whatever it was that obviously had her so frustrated.

"If I tell you something, will you promise not to tell anyone else?"

She hesitated. This was her best friend's daughter offering to confide something that her mother probably didn't know, something that maybe Kristin needed to know. On the other hand, Kristin had enough to worry about right now and Katie obviously needed someone to talk to. "Okay."

"Promise."

"I promise," Jess said.

Katie took a deep breath and then blurted out, "I was going to have sex with him tonight."

Jess was suddenly grateful she was sitting down because the matter-of-fact statement could have knocked her over.

She had no idea what to say, how to handle this. Obviously the girl needed someone to talk to, but surely she had to know someone more qualified than a woman who had, until very recently, only been a transient presence in her life.

"I had condoms," Kate continued. "I thought I was smart and prepared and ready…and then I started to have doubts. I feel like such an idiot."

"Don't." On this point she felt justified in being firm. "Don't ever apologize for the way you feel. And don't ever try to force yourself to do something you're not comfortable doing just for someone else."

"But what if he dumps me now?"

Jess thought of Jake's friend, the boy she and Nick had played basketball with, the boy who looked at Katie as if the sun rose and set with her. "I don't think he will," she said gently. "But if he does, then he wasn't the right guy for you."

"That's so lame."

She shrugged. "Maybe so, but it's also true."

"It was actually Ethan's idea to wait," Katie admitted. "He said I was too young. But I'm not a kid. I don't want

Ethan to treat me like a kid. And I know he's had sex before, so why doesn't he want to have it with me?"

Jess often wondered what kind of parent she'd have been, if she'd had a child of her own. She'd imagined mixing the ingredients to bake cookies together, snuggling to read stories at bedtime, maybe wiping a few tears and bandaging scraped knees. She'd never imagined this kind of teenage angst.

"I have to admit, I feel completely unprepared to answer that question."

Katie huffed out an impatient breath. "I bet he did it with that girl who was all over him at Walton's."

"Is that what you want to be, Katie—just another girl he did it with?"

"No." She pouted for a moment, then asked, "When did you lose your virginity?"

Maybe Jess should have been shocked by the bold question. Instead, she thought of Nick and she smiled. "I was older than you."

"How much older?"

"A lot."

Katie's gaze narrowed suspiciously.

"Okay, I was seventeen," Jess admitted. "But it wasn't just my age that made the difference—it was the guy."

"Did you love him?"

"With my whole heart."

Katie sighed. "I love Ethan, and I don't want to lose him. And I thought that if we had sex, he'd stand by me regardless."

"Regardless of what?"

"The possibility that Jake will kill him if he finds out we've been seeing each other."

Jess smiled. "I don't think Ethan will scare away that easily. But I also think Jake—and your parents—will be less concerned about your relationship with Ethan if you stop sneaking around."

"Maybe."

"You said you had condoms," Jess remembered suddenly, an uncomfortable suspicion gnawing at the back of her mind.

Katie nodded.

"Where did you get them?"

The girl tipped her head forward, hiding behind the curtain of her hair. "From…um…my dad's dresser."

Jess didn't know whether to laugh or groan as her suspicion was confirmed. "Didn't you worry that he might notice they were missing?"

"What does he need them for? It's not as if him and mom ever have sex."

Jess remained silent, letting the girl mull that one over for a moment.

"Oh," she said at last. "I guess if they didn't use them, he wouldn't have them."

She nodded.

"I'll put them back."

"That's probably a good idea. But if you think you will need some—not that I'm encouraging you to have sex with Ethan," Jess hastened to add, "but it's smart to be prepared—then I'll take you to the drugstore to get some."

Katie looked horrified by the prospect. "I can't even buy tampons at the drugstore without everyone in town knowing the brand before I even get home."

An exaggeration, Jess was sure, but the possibility of being seen buying condoms would definitely rate some major embarrassment for a teenage girl. "I'll buy them," she said. "Now go put those condoms back and go to bed. We have a busy day tomorrow."

"Okay." Katie kissed her cheek. "Thanks, Aunt Jess."

"Good night, Katie."

She heard the creak of the door as it opened and closed, then sighed into the darkness. Katie might be grateful for the offer, but Jess doubted that Kristin would be. She was suddenly glad she'd promised Katie not to tell anyone about their conversation. It would be one less thing to rock the shaky foundation of her renewed friendship with Kristin.

Jess and Nick took the kids to visit Caleb on Saturday. Jess took advantage of the chaotic family reunion to commandeer Kristin away from the hospital for a few hours.

"I don't even like shopping," Kristin protested, as she was dragged by the arm and out of the hospital.

"Have you ever been to Macy's?" Jess asked.

"No, but—"

"Then you've never been shopping." She took her sunglasses out of her pocket, settled them on her nose.

"I shouldn't go too far. What if—"

"You needed to get out of that room for a while," she insisted. "And Brian has my cell number if he needs to get in touch with you."

"You should be taking Katie instead. She loves to shop."

"Another time. Today you need a chance to recharge your batteries, and I needed an opportunity to speak to you alone."

"Oh." Typical of Kristin, she ceased protesting when she thought it was about someone else. "Is something wrong?"

"No." Jess stopped at her favorite corner café. "Have you ever had a pumpkin spice latte?"

"What?"

She grinned and tugged her friend through the door. "Come on."

A few minutes later, they were settled at a table by the window with a couple of lattes and biscotti. "When I first moved to New York, I used to get such a kick out of sitting and watching the people."

"I don't imagine you have much time for that now."

"Not usually," Jess admitted.

"Did I ever thank you for taking the time to stay with Jake and Katie?"

"You don't have to thank me—I wanted to help." Still, she was pleased by Kristin's acknowledgment and hoped it was another sign of their friendship growing stronger again.

"But I know it couldn't have been easy to reorganize your work schedule."

Jess waved off the comment. "I didn't bring you here to talk about work."

"But there was something you wanted to talk about," Kristin guessed. "This wasn't just about getting me out of the hospital."

"You haven't been outside in days," she said. "But you're right—there was something." Still she hesitated, uncertain how to broach a decidedly awkward topic.

"Is this about Nick?"

"No."

"Oh. When you came up together, I thought maybe…"

Jess shook her head and decided, as reluctant as she was to broach the subject of the missing birth control, she wanted to talk about Kristin's brother even less. "I solved the mystery of the lost condoms."

Kristin's hand shook as she set down her mug. "And?"

"It wasn't Brian."

"Oh." She exhaled a long, slow breath. "Are you sure?"

"Positive."

"Then who—"

Jess shook her head. "Please don't ask me."

Kristin broke off a piece of biscotti. "Katie," she said softly, and closed her eyes on a sigh. "If Jake needed condoms, he'd buy them from a vending machine in the bathroom at school."

"They sell condoms at the high school?"

"It's a new millennium, Jess." She shook her head. "But Katie would worry that someone might see her and tell someone else and, well, you know how rumors get started. I had no idea that she—I can't believe it—she's only fifteen—"

"She didn't use them," Jess interrupted. She winced at the betrayal of Katie's confidence, but Kristin was already convinced that her daughter was the culprit and the truth was less damaging than what she was obviously thinking. "There, uh, there was no reason to."

"Thank God. I'm so not ready for that."

"I think she realized that she isn't ready for it, either."

"She talked to you about this?"

"A little."

"She never talks to me about stuff like this. Anytime I try to start a conversation, she just rolls her eyes and says 'They teach this stuff in school, you know, Mom.'"

"Did you want to talk to your mom about sex?" Jess asked.

"No. It was awkward and embarrassing—for both of us." Kristin sighed again. "I guess I should be grateful, at least, that Katie talked to you. Except that now I have to track down Ethan and kill him."

"You know that she's been seeing him?"

"I obviously didn't notice how close they'd gotten."

"At least she's being smart."

"I know that should make me feel better," Kristin admitted. "But it doesn't."

"Maybe this will make you feel better." Jess pushed an envelope across the table.

"What's that?"

"Your itinerary for tonight—theater tickets, dinner reservations and hotel keys."

"I can't go out tonight. I have to—"

"You don't have to do anything except spend some quality time with your husband and Jake and Katie."

"But Caleb—"

"I've already talked to Nick. He and I will stay with Caleb tonight. There are four tickets to one of the latest Broadway hits, reservations for dinner at Sardi's after the show, and at the Courtland hotel for an overnight stay."

Kristin was visibly stunned. "I can't believe you did all of this. I don't know what to say."

Jess smiled. "Say 'thank you, I'm sure we'll have a wonderful time.' By the way, I booked adjoining rooms at the hotel. That way the kids will be close, but you and Brian will still have privacy. Maybe you can talk, sort some things out between you."

"I don't know, Jess. We haven't communicated in so long, I'm not sure we even know how to anymore."

"You need to try." She thought of Jake and Katie and Caleb and how devastated they would be if their parents split up. "You've got so much at stake, so much to lose. You can't give up until you've tried everything. And knowing Brian hasn't been unfaithful to you has to relieve some of the tension you've been feeling."

"It does," Kristin admitted. "Thank you for telling me, and for being there for Katie. She's obviously dealing with a lot of stuff right now—and she needs two parents to support her."

She looked at Jess with the familiar glint of determination shining in her eyes. "I'm going to talk to him. Tonight I'll tell Brian how I've been feeling and see what we can do about it."

"Good idea," Jess agreed. "But first you need to finish up your latte—we have some serious shopping to do."

Caleb's eyes were closed, his chest rising and falling with the steady rhythm of his breathing. Nick was so pleased to see his nephew without the tube in his throat, looking like a normal seven-year-old boy again.

"I think he's asleep," he said.

Jess leaned back in her chair, propped her feet on the frame of Caleb's bed, and closed her eyes. "Finally. I would have gone cross-eyed if I'd had to play another game with that crazy hedgehog."

"You were the one who bought him the system," he reminded her.

She shrugged. "You can't expect a kid to stay entertained all day with only a television."

"It seems to me you emptied out the entire toy department. Look at all these books and games and that ridiculous stuffed frog."

Her eyes flew open. "That stuffed frog is not ridiculous, it's cute. And Caleb loved it."

He couldn't deny that. In fact, the oversize lime green creature was tucked beside Caleb in his bed right now.

"You spoiled him. All of them." In addition to the gifts she'd purchased for Caleb, she'd given Katie a Macy's gift certificate along with an open invitation to visit for a weekend shopping excursion, and she'd stunned Jake with courtside seats for a Knicks game.

"I don't get to see them very often." Her tone held a wistfulness that surprised him.

"Is that going to change now?"

She hesitated. "I don't know. I'd like to say that I'll make a point of visiting more often, but the truth is, my schedule at work can be really chaotic."

He considered challenging her choice of priorities but didn't want to destroy the comfortable rapport they'd so recently established. Instead he said, "It was a really nice thing you did for Kristin and Brian tonight."

She turned her head to look at him. "Are you saying I'm nice?"

He laughed. "Doing something nice and being nice aren't always the same thing. But yes, for the record, I do think you're nice."

"Does that mean I'll never get to see you naked?"

"It's not the same. For a woman to see a man naked, she generally only has to ask."

"I seem to recall that I did ask, and my request was denied."

"Not denied," he protested. "Just deferred."

"Why?"

"Because if we're going to have a relationship, we need a chance to get to know each other. Not as the teenagers we once were, but as the adults we are now."

She eyed him warily. "I didn't think you wanted a relationship. I thought you wanted sex."

He didn't know whether to laugh or throttle her for being so obtuse. "I'm thirty-eight years old, Jess. I want more than just sex."

She frowned.

"Does that change things for you?"

"Maybe."

"Why?"

"Because a relationship requires a lot more time and effort to maintain it."

"Or maybe you're just afraid."

"This has been fun, Freud, but I'm too tired to argue with you right now."

"We're not arguing, we're discussing your tendency to shy away from an adult relationship."

"I said I'd have sex with you. Isn't that adult enough?"

"Now you're trying to distract me."

"Is it working?"

He laughed. "Yeah."

He reached into the bag of snacks they'd brought to sustain them through the night and pulled out a can of Coke. "You want one?"

Shifting in her chair, she stifled a yawn. "No, thanks."

He popped the top, took a long swallow. "Kristin said you stopped by your office while you were out this afternoon."

Jess shrugged. "I thought it was a good idea, since I was in town anyway, to see if there was anything that needed immediate attention."

"You miss it, don't you?"

"I've enjoyed the break, but yes, I miss working. That's when I feel that I have a purpose, that I'm doing something important."

"Staying with Jake and Katie was important to Kristin. Helping out in my office was important to me."

"But both of those arrangements are only temporary. My work at Dawson, Murray & Neale is…"

"Your life?" he supplied.

"Yeah," she admitted.

"I've been accused of burying myself in my work, too."

"Sometimes there isn't a choice," she said. "I'm sure it's the same in your job—there are expectations and deadlines and the threat of penalties."

"Have you ever failed to meet a deadline?"

She smiled. "No."

"Because you'll work around the clock to ensure that doesn't happen."

She nodded.

"I've done the same thing," he confessed. "Canceled plans, stayed up all night. Maybe we have more in common than you realize."

"You mean because we're both single-minded?"

"Focused," he amended. "And dedicated and reliable."

She grimaced. "I'm glad you stopped before you got to boring."

He wasn't about to let her comment sidetrack him from his point. "We also have a strong desire to succeed—that's got to be a positive thing for a long-term relationship."

"Putting two workaholics together is a recipe for disaster," she countered.

He nearly groaned in frustration.

How could he convince her she was wrong? What words could possibly motivate her to stop fighting him on this?

Or maybe that was the problem. Jess had always believed in fighting for something that mattered. And for the first time, he had an idea about how to break their apparent deadlock.

"You're right," he agreed. "Relationships require a lot of work. I know I'm up for the challenge. The question is, are you?"

Jess was beginning to wonder if she and Nick were ever going to sleep together. He didn't really seem to be losing interest. He was still attentive and flirty and he still kissed her as though there was no tomorrow. But it never went any further than that.

It was both fascinating and frustrating to realize that he was taking his time to get to know her rather than pushing her into bed when they both knew it was where she wanted to be. Instead, he'd decided he wanted a relationship and was determined to build one.

Not that she really objected to the idea of something more than a transitional involvement—she just had too many doubts about how, or if, it would work. But she went along with Nick's plan because she enjoyed spending time with him, getting to know him again, and because she realized they had missed out on a lot by rushing into sex so many years ago.

Holding hands, cuddling together in front of the television, stealing kisses inside a dark movie theater—she regretted that they'd bypassed those.

She also regretted that they didn't have more time. Although the doctors were pleased with Caleb's recovery, they still had no idea when he would be coming home. Jess had to be back at work the following Monday morning and, as it was now Tuesday, that meant there were only five more days until she had to leave.

As anxious as she was to get back to her life in Man-

hattan, she knew she was going to miss Kristin's family—
and especially Nick—when she was gone. But she said
nothing to him about her impending date of departure,
choosing instead to simply enjoy the time they were spending together.

Tonight he'd said he would pick her up at eight, although he'd given no hint of any plans he'd made for the
evening except to tell her to dress casual. So she'd put on
the only pair of jeans she'd brought and topped them with
a short-sleeved yellow sweater.

"Where are we going?" Jess asked when she noticed he
was driving toward the outskirts of town.

He merely smiled, an enigmatic curving of his lips that
both intrigued and worried her. "You'll see."

"Not that I don't appreciate the effort you're making,"
she said. "But we're both adults who want the same thing.
Why are we playing these games?"

"Because we never played them together when we were
teenagers." He grinned. "And because they're fun."

"I only ever played basketball when I was in high school."

"That's right—serious Jessica. Always practicing,
studying or working."

"I needed a scholarship if I was going to go to college."

He shook his head. "Let's forget about that for now.
Let's just go back in time and pretend there's nothing to
worry about but the here and now."

She saw the sign for the drive-in overhead, laughed. "I
think the only thing showing is Closed For The Season."

"I'm hoping the windows will be so steamed up we
wouldn't be able to watch a movie anyway." He steered into a clearing in front of the oversized screen and shifted
into Park. "I really want to kiss you, Jess."

She released the clasp of her seat belt and met him half-way—at the center console.

Nick cursed at the obstruction. "Back seat."

Jess obeyed without question. Her heart was hammering against her ribs. She'd been waiting for this moment, anticipating it. But now that it was here, she felt as jittery as a seventeen-year-old out past curfew.

Somehow, while she'd been pondering these thoughts, he'd managed to slide her sweater up and whisk it over her head.

Then he kissed her, hungrily, greedily, as if he were famished and she were a feast. He nipped at her bottom lip, plunged deep into her mouth. She responded with the same intensity, the same need.

Then he tore his lips from hers to trail hot kisses down her throat, across her collarbone, over the curve of her breast. Her skin tingled everywhere he touched, frissons of pleasure streaking to the center of her being.

His mouth found one already peaked nipple and suckled hard through the lace of her bra.

She gasped. "I…I thought you wanted to take it slow."

He unfastened her bra, slipped it down her arms and tossed it aside. "Six days is slow enough."

Eighteen years and six days, she thought.

Then he turned his attention back to her breasts, his mouth hot and wet against her flesh, and her thoughts were swept away on a wave of pure pleasure.

He lowered her down onto the seat, the cool leather a welcome contrast to her heated skin.

He found the button at the front of her jeans, popped it open, slid the zipper down. Every muscle in her body tensed as his hand moved over her belly, then lower.

His fingers dipped beneath the edge of her lace panties. She felt the throbbing between her thighs, as he slid a finger into the slick heat and hummed his approval.

He rubbed his thumb over the aching nub at the apex of her thighs—a feather-light caress, more a tease than a touch.

"Nick." It was a whimper, a plea.

He pushed her jeans over her hips, anxious to feel her naked body pressed against his, then started to strip away his clothes. He pulled his shirt over his head, cursing as his elbow banged against the side window. "Damn, I'm too old for this. Maybe we should go back to my place."

"Next time," she said, reaching for the buckle of his belt.

"Seriously, Jess, I—"

Whatever he'd planned to say was lost in a haze as her hand cupped his arousal through the denim, her fingers sliding and tightening against the length of him. He groaned.

"I've learned a thing or two in the past eighteen years," she told him, unfastening the button fly with a quick flick of her wrist.

"Now's not a good time to be flaunting your sexual exploits with other men."

"I wasn't intending to share any of the details." She pushed his jeans and briefs down. "Only to show you how you might benefit."

"Jess." He growled the warning.

She wrapped her fingers around him, without any barriers this time, and his eyes nearly crossed with lust.

"Still want to wait until we can get back to your place?" she teased.

Hell, no. He'd be lucky if he could wait another five seconds.

He grabbed her around the waist and lifted her so that she was straddling his lap. He started to reach for the condom he'd taken from his pocket, but she grabbed it first. Then she slowly rolled it into place while Nick closed his eyes and said a quick mental prayer that he wouldn't erupt like a novice and embarrass himself.

The last time they'd been together he'd been a twenty-year-old with more enthusiasm than finesse. Although Jessica hadn't complained about either his technique or endurance, he was hoping to give her an experience tonight that would not just obliterate her memories of that awkward first time, but the memories of all her other lovers. But to do that, he had to stay in control—for more than thirty seconds.

Once the condom was in place, she settled over him, hovering so that he was positioned at the juncture of her thighs. She lowered herself a few inches, took the tip of him inside her slick heat, then slowly withdrew.

His hands gripped the edge of the leather seat and sweat broke out on his brow as she moved down and then away again.

"You're playing a dangerous game," he warned.

"You're the one who insisted that games were fun."

She pressed her lips against his as she descended again, just a little farther this time. Her tongue slid into his mouth and out again, mirroring the slow motion of their bodies. It was bold and erotic, and it was driving him crazy.

Two, he decided, could play this game.

Tearing his mouth from hers, he leaned forward to take the rosy tip of one breast in his mouth and suckled deeply. He cupped her other breast in his hand, rolling the nipple between his thumb and finger.

She moaned, arched toward him, the action driving him deeper inside her but still not deep enough.

While his mouth continued to tease her breasts, alternating from one to the other, he slid a hand between their bodies, searching and finding the tiny nub in the nest of soft curls. He brushed his thumb over it, heard her gasp, felt her quiver.

"Nick."

He loved the way she said his name, in a low, throaty murmur. He loved the way she responded to him touching her, moving inside her.

Her fingers were digging into his shoulders now, the short nails biting into his flesh. He stroked her in slow, seductive circles, listening to the changing patterns of her breathing as he pushed her closer and closer to the peak of pleasure. When he knew that she was teetering on the edge, he drove himself into her and felt the pulsing flood of heat as she cried out and climaxed around him.

He gritted his teeth, fought for control, but the waves of her release battered his restraint and tossed him into a swirling vortex of pleasure.

Chapter Thirteen

Jessica's body was limp against his, her head nestled in the crook of his shoulder, her mind completely, blissfully blank. She sighed happily, snuggled closer.

His fingers traced a lazy path along her spine. "I think it's time to take you home."

"I don't think I can move right now."

"Because I've exhausted you sexually or because it's crowded in here?"

She smiled against his throat. "Definitely the first option."

"Definitely?"

She lifted her head to meet the smug satisfaction in his gaze. She was feeling too satisfied herself to take offense.

"Definitely," she confirmed, then pressed her lips to his. She felt a stirring between her thighs, wriggled against him.

Nick groaned. "I don't know whether to be proud or

ashamed of the fact that you make me feel like I'm twenty years old again."

"Personally, I'm grateful," she teased.

"Personally, I think I'm too old to be having sex in the back seat."

"There's no way we could have done it in the front—with the console and steering wheel in the way."

"Can't argue with that," he agreed.

"And it was your idea to relive the dates we never had in high school."

"I guess it was." He found her sweater on the floor, tugged it over her head.

Jess slipped her arms into the sleeves. "So, was this, uh, a frequent occurrence for you in high school?"

"Sex in the back seat? Or sex at the drive-in?"

"Either."

He grinned. "Not frequent."

"But you've done this before?"

"Not in this vehicle and never with you," he said, brushing his lips against hers. "Never with anyone who makes me feel the way you do."

She huffed out an exasperated breath. "Is that supposed to appease me?"

"Do you need to be appeased?"

She shouldn't. Whatever he'd done in high school had happened before they'd ever been together, and since then, they had eighteen years of history apart from one another. But it was surprising how proprietary she was feeling now that they'd been intimate again. And how uncomfortable it made her to realize that she could feel proprietary. She'd gone into this with her eyes open, knowing that whatever might happen between her and Nick could only be temporary. Her life was in New York; his was here. The geographical distance and diversity of their lifestyles weren't easy barriers to breach, even if they wanted to.

"I have no right to ask you those kinds of questions."

"We just made love, Jess. I'd say that gives you certain rights."

She sighed. "Maybe it frustrates me, just a little, that so many of my firsts are with you, and all of yours are with other women."

"Not all of them."

She looked at him skeptically.

"You were the first girl I ever loved."

She was silent.

"And you were the first girl to ask me about sex—at least for fact-finding purposes."

Twenty years later, Jess still flushed at the memory. "I had no one else to talk to."

"How about your gym teacher or a guidance counselor or your mother?"

"I never felt as comfortable with any of them as I felt with you."

"Well, I have to admit the conversation made me very *un*comfortable."

"But I knew you were having sex with Ellen Webster, so you were the perfect person to talk to."

He thought of Ellen with fond recollection: blond hair, green eyes, lush breasts and a reputation—well-deserved—for being hotter and faster than Tony DeMarco's fire-engine-red classic five-speed Camaro. Then he remembered Jess's question and frowned. "How did you know about me and Ellen?"

"Everyone knew about you and Ellen."

His frown deepened.

"And I needed a guy's opinion."

"I couldn't stand to think that you were even thinking about sex," he admitted. "It killed me to think of any other guy putting his hands on you."

"You know you were the first."

"But not the last."

"Actually, 'last' meaning 'most recent,' you are."

He smiled. "I wish it was 'last' meaning 'only.' I know it's crazy, but I can't stand the thought of you being with anyone else."

"At the risk of further inflating your already over-inflated ego, I can tell you that no one has ever made me feel the way you do."

He cupped her face in his palms and kissed her, slowly, tenderly. "Same goes."

It was strange for Jess to be at Nick's office, the day after having sex with him, and trying to pretend it had never happened. The fact that Nick wasn't there should have made it less awkward. Instead, his absence made her doubts grow.

He'd called in to say that he was on-site and would be in the office later, but she couldn't be sure that he wasn't avoiding her. Had she been too pushy? Was he sorry they'd had sex? Was that why he'd arranged to be out of the office today?

She propped her elbows on her desk and buried her face in her hands. This was crazy. She was an independent career woman suddenly plagued by fears and insecurities, and it wasn't a comfortable feeling.

She'd never felt like this in New York. Even when she'd

found out her husband was cheating on her, she hadn't fallen into this pit of self-doubt. Because she hadn't just been a jilted wife, she'd been a jilted wife with a successful career and a promising future.

She wanted to go back to Manhattan. She wanted to go into her office, sit in her leather chair behind her polished antique desk and feel important.

And why shouldn't she?

Caleb was well on his way to a full recovery and would be coming home soon. Kristin wouldn't be expecting her to stay. There was absolutely no reason she couldn't get into her car right now and go.

No reason except that Nick was here—which was exactly the kind of thinking that had gotten her into trouble so many years before.

"That was a heartfelt sigh."

She glanced up, forced a smile. "Hi, Mason. I didn't hear you come in."

"You were obviously deep in thought."

"Don't tell the boss—I'm supposed to be deep in work."

"Somehow I don't think he'll fire you. Not when I'm guessing that you're the reason he was walking around the site this morning with a stupid grin on his face."

His statement went a long way toward alleviating her doubts and she couldn't hold back her own smile.

"Like that," Mason said.

"Was there any particular reason you stopped by?"

"Yeah, Nick asked me to pick up the Leonard file."

She pulled open the K to P drawer. "Is he still at the site?"

He took the folder from her hand and nodded. "He said to let you know he hoped to be back by lunch."

"Okay."

But Mason didn't seem to be in any hurry to leave, instead propping a hip against the corner of her desk. "Nick and I have known each other a long time," he said. "Not as long as you and he, but still a long time."

"I know he considers you a friend as well as a business partner," she said cautiously.

"I was the best man at his wedding."

"Oh."

"Because friends stick by their friends, even when they know they're making a mistake."

"You didn't like Tina?" She couldn't imagine any man with a pulse who wouldn't have been impressed by Nick's ex-wife.

"I didn't dislike her," he said. "I just knew that she wasn't right for Nick."

"Obviously he thought otherwise."

"Not for long."

"I'm sure there's a point to this, but—"

"The point is that you could be right for him. Or you could break his heart."

"Nick and I both understand what is—and what is not—happening between us."

"Are you sure about that?"

She'd thought so, but now she wondered. And while part of her wanted to be annoyed by his questions, she knew he was genuinely concerned about his friend. So all she said was, "You're a nice guy, Mason."

He cringed.

The reaction was so similar to Nick's response to the same compliment, she couldn't help but laugh.

She was still smiling when Nick came through the door. He glanced from her to his partner, who was still perched on the corner of her desk. "What are you doing here, Sullivan?"

Mason grinned broadly. "Just making conversation."

"More like making the moves—on my woman."

"Your woman, huh?" Mason winked at her.

Jess opened her mouth to protest the title. The protest died when Nick leaned down to cover her lips with his own.

His kiss was hot and hungry with absolutely no regard for the fact that they weren't alone in the office. In two seconds, Jess forgot as well.

"An innocent bystander could get singed by all that heat you two are generating," Mason complained.

"There's nothing innocent about you," Nick said. "But if you're concerned, feel free to leave."

"I'm going. And I'm locking the door on my way out."

"Good plan."

Then Nick pulled her up out of her chair and started kissing her again, and the last of her doubts about last night vanished.

"I've been thinking about you all day," he said.

"It's only eleven o'clock," she pointed out.

"I've been up since five."

"Why?"

"Because I had to be at the site by six."

She slid her arms around his neck. "Is there anywhere you have to be now?"

"I know where I *want* to be," he said. "And who I want to be with, but I have to go shopping."

"Shopping?"

"For balloons and other decoration kind of things."

"Why?" she asked again.

He grinned. "Because Caleb's coming home tonight."

* * *

Despite the short notice, Jess and Nick managed—with Jake and Katie's help—to get the house in shape for Caleb's welcome home party.

It was almost five o'clock when Katie shouted from the living room, "They're here."

Jess took a last look around to make sure everything was in place while the others went outside to meet Kristin and Brian and Caleb.

She hovered in the background as hugs and kisses were exchanged all around, pleased to see that while Caleb was moving slowly, he was doing so without help. And apart from a small patch of hair shaved off of his head, he looked none the worse for his ordeal.

As he came through to the living room, he was chatting away with his parents, negotiating for time to play video games.

"An hour a day," Brian reminded him of the rule.

"But I haven't played in twelve days, so I should get twelve hours today."

His mother held up her fingers and began counting off her objections. "First, Aunt Jess bought you a Game Boy when you were in the hospital, so you haven't been completely deprived. Second, there aren't twelve hours left in today. And third, there is no way I'm letting you sit and stare at a television screen for twelve hours."

"Ah, Mom."

"You can have an extra half hour once a week until you've made up the hours," she told him. "Then it's back down to an hour a day."

"But that'll take—" his brows drew together "—twenty-four weeks."

"Good math skills," Jess noted.

"They'd be even better if he spent less time in front of the television."

"But that's almost a *year*," Caleb protested.

"Twenty-four weeks is six months," Kristin told him. "Half a year."

Their argument was interrupted by the doorbell.

"Pizza," Jess told them, as Nick went to answer the door.

"With olives?" Caleb asked hopefully, the argument about video games temporarily forgotten.

"There is one with pepperoni and olives," she said.

They ate at the dining room table, the mood joyful and celebratory. Everyone talked at the same time, carrying on various conversations through and around one another. It was chaotic and fun and Jess was pleased to be sharing in it.

When the pizza was all gone and Caleb was starting to yawn, Jess got up from the table to get dessert. Nick followed her with an armload of dirty dishes.

She helped him load the dishwasher then got out the dessert plates and forks while Nick went downstairs to get the cake.

She found matches in the cupboard and lit one, then hesitated as she stared at the seven candles.

"What's the matter?"

"I'm having second thoughts about this now," she admitted. "Maybe I should have run out to the bakery and…"

"Caleb was wondering if we had any ice cream," Kristin said, coming into the kitchen. Her gaze dropped to the cake. "Oh."

Jess shifted. "I'm sorry. I should have talked to you before—"

Kristin shook her head, her eyes shining with tears. "He asked for his cake. When he woke up, it was almost the first thing he mentioned."

Jess felt an overwhelming sense of relief that she'd finally got something right, even if her choice of birthday present had been all wrong.

Nick took the plates and forks and slipped quietly from the room. Kristin turned to Jess. "I'd assumed it had been thrown out." Her voice was thick with emotion.

"I could tell you'd put a lot of effort into making it," Jess said softly.

Kristin smiled. "All he wanted was an R2-D2 cake, and I was so afraid I was going to screw it up."

"It's perfect."

Her friend wiped a tear from her cheek. "Thank you. Not just for the cake, but for everything. It's been a long couple of weeks and although I still wish none of it had happened, I'm glad to have you back in my life."

Jess hugged her. "Me, too."

"I wanted to thank you, too, for the night out in New York. Brian and I needed to spend some time with Jake and Katie. And when we got back to the hotel, I took your advice."

"You talked to Brian?"

Kristin nodded. "It turns out that neither of us has really been happy, not for a long time. But we also talked about the reasons why, what each of us wants from our marriage, and we realized the one thing that hasn't changed over the years is that we still love each other."

"I'm glad," Jess said softly.

Kristin smiled. "Me, too. We talked through the night, almost until the sun came up. And then—" her cheeks flushed prettily, her voice dropped to a whisper "—we made love." Her smile widened. "And it was incredible."

"Okay—those are details I don't need to know."

"I used to tell you everything when we were younger." Jess nodded.

"I've missed that, having someone I could talk to about anything. Someone who would understand me and not judge me. I was glad you finally told me why it was so hard for you to come back here. But in my heart, I was still angry." Kristin wiped her eyes and went on.

"One of the things I realized after talking with Brian, is that I need to express my thoughts and feelings. I was mad at you for not anticipating needs that I never shared with you. And I was so busy playing the part of the injured party I didn't see that you needed me. I just hope we can both forgive our mistakes and move forward."

Jess nodded. "I'd like that."

"Good." Kristin smiled. "Now let's light these candles and have cake."

Jess laughed, her heart feeling lighter than it had in years. Today was truly a day for celebrations. Caleb was home. Kristin and Brian had renewed their commitment to one another. Jess and Kristin were giving their friendship a clean slate. And tonight, she would be celebrating in Nick's arms.

Kristin asked Jessica to carry the cake out to the table. It seemed fitting, since Jessica was the reason they had the cake for their celebration, and it gave Kristin a chance to see the joy light up Caleb's face when he spotted it.

He'd been thrilled with the cake and ate two servings, both with ice cream. Afterward, he was yawning profusely and trying valiantly to stop his eyes from drifting shut.

Brian offered to take him upstairs to help him get ready for bed. Noting the hour, Jake begged a ride to work from Nick so he wouldn't be late for his shift at the grocery story, leaving Katie to help her mom and Jess clean up.

When the last traces of the celebration had been cleared away, Katie disappeared into her room with a novel and Jess excused herself to check her e-mail.

Kristin stood in the kitchen, feeling blissfully free of stress and worry, and yet somehow at a loss as to what to do. Since the accident, her life had been consumed with Caleb—sitting with him, praying for him, worrying about him. Now it was eight o'clock on a Wednesday night and she had no idea what to do.

Brian came into the room a few minutes later. "Caleb was asleep before I finished pulling up the covers."

"He had a busy day."

He slid an arm around her waist and she leaned her head back against his shoulder, breathing in his familiar masculine scent.

"It was a good day, though," he said. "For all of us."

She nodded. "And it was good to hear laughter in the house again."

"I've missed that," he admitted. "And I've missed you."

"We're finally home now." She knew he'd understand that she wasn't just talking about their physical location but the progress they'd made on a personal level.

"Yeah, we are." He pressed his lips to her temple. "So why were you frowning when I came into the room?"

"I was just trying to remember what I should be doing. Everything in all of our lives has been turned upside down since Caleb's accident—I feel so disconnected from the usual routines."

"I think it's time to shake up the usual routines."

"What did you have in mind?"

He turned her around so that she was facing him. "Let's start with this," he said, and kissed her. Softly, slowly, and very thoroughly.

"Kris—oops!"

She pulled away in time to see Jessica backpedaling quickly out of the room.

"Sorry," her friend said. "I just…um…I'm going to go out…for a while."

Then she was gone.

Kristin buried her face in Brian's shirt.

"There's no reason to be embarrassed," he told her. "We are married, you know."

"With two of our three kids in the house," she pointed out.

"You want to stop?"

She shook her head. "I want to go upstairs."

"Your wish—" he said, sweeping her off her feet and into his arms "—is my command."

She giggled. "You don't have to carry me, Brian."

"Yes, I do," he said. "Because now that I have you in my arms, I don't ever intend to let you go."

It was a foolishly romantic thing to say, but it made her heart flutter wildly inside her breast.

"I love you, Brian."

He smiled down at her. "I love you, too, and I'm going to prove it to you every chance I get."

Jessica slipped out the front door and caught Nick as he was coming up the driveway. She took him by the arm and steered him away. "We need to go out for a while."

"A while?"

"Your sister and brother-in-law need some privacy." She started toward the back of the property, leading the way toward his house.

"I don't want to know," he said.

She smiled. "Don't want to know that they were making out in the kitchen like a couple of teenagers?"

"I'd rather think about the time that you and I ended up the same way."

"Maybe it's the room."

"Or maybe not." He stopped abruptly in the cover of the trees and crushed his mouth down on hers in a brief but potent kiss. "Because I seem to have this irresistible urge to kiss you anywhere and anytime."

"I have no objection to you giving in to that urge."

"No?" He kissed her again.

And again.

Until she was breathless and dizzy and filled with the sweet, gentle ache of wanting.

"As much as I've always liked this spot, I was hoping maybe we could go back to my place tonight."

"I thought you'd never ask."

He grinned. "I wasn't asking. If I had to, I was going to kidnap you and take you away to have my wicked way with you."

"Wicked?" She smiled, intrigued by the idea. "I'll race you to the house."

And she started to run, skirting around the trees, over the creek and through Nick's yard.

She knew he could beat her if he tried. But he let her keep the lead almost until she'd reached the back door of his house, then he swept her off her feet. She was breathless and laughing when he dragged her over the threshold.

"Take me upstairs, Nick."

He pressed a brief kiss to her lips. "Give me five minutes."

"I'm hoping it will take a little longer than that," she teased.

The look he sent her caused her pulse to scramble. "Count on it."

He was back in less than the five minutes he'd asked for and scooped her into his arms again.

"Put me down, Nick."

"I thought you wanted me to take you upstairs."

"I meant 'lead' not 'carry.'"

"I want to carry you," he said. "It's romantic."

"Not if you throw your back out before we make it to the bed."

He chuckled as he started up the steps. "I promise you, that is *not* going to happen."

Her breath caught in her throat as he carried her through an open doorway. He set her gently back on her feet, and she turned in a slow circle to look around the room. There were candles, dozens of candles, their flickering light the only illumination in the room. Crystal vases filled with roses, the petals in varying shades of pink and red, their sweet fragrance scenting the air. And a silver ice bucket with a bottle inside and two long-stemmed flutes at the ready.

It was a scene set for seduction: totally extravagant, completely unnecessary and absolutely perfect.

"Oh, Nick."

"I wanted to give you all the romance we've missed out on."

She hadn't thought she wanted or needed romance. Because no one had ever given it to her before. But now Nick had, and her heart simply melted.

She turned and kissed him. "It's beautiful."

He brushed the back of his knuckles down her cheek. "You're beautiful, Jess."

There was something in his gaze, something dark and compelling that made her wary as much as it made her yearn. She tried not to think about what it meant, what she wanted it to mean, and stay focused on the here and now.

She started to maneuver him toward the bed. Because as much as she appreciated all this romance, what she really wanted was Nick. Naked and sweaty and buried deep inside her.

But Nick stepped away, moving across the room to pick up the bottle of wine. "You always like to be in control, don't you, Jess?"

"I just know what I want." She slid her hands up his back, smiled when he nearly bobbled the wine. "I want you, Nick."

He turned, pressed a glass into her hand. "Have you ever heard of heightening the anticipation?"

She sipped. "You're complicating things."

"And you wanted to keep them simple."

"I thought we both did."

"You thought wrong."

Chapter Fourteen

Jessica felt the first spurt of panic through her system.

Then Nick pressed his lips to the side of her neck and she shivered, forgetting everything else but how much she wanted to be with him.

She reached for the buttons on his shirt. He grasped her hand, held it behind her back.

"Not yet," he told her.

"Why?"

He smiled at the frustration evident in her tone. "Because I want to touch you first. I want to spend a long time just touching you. I want to feel you tremble and hear you sigh."

The heated promise of his words turned the gentle ache inside her to raging need. But she wanted to touch him, too. She wanted to run her hands and her lips over every inch of his body, absorbing his texture and his taste. And locking the memory inside her forever.

She gulped down the rest of her wine, set her glass aside. "What are you waiting for?"

He smiled and placed his half-empty glass beside hers. "I want to watch you, too. I want to see your eyes darken with passion and your heart race." He touched a fingertip to the throbbing pulse point at the base of her jaw and smiled. "There are all manner of things I want to see and do with you, Jess."

The hand that had been monitoring her pulse skimmed down her throat, over the swell of her breast, his knuckles brushing over her nipple. Her breath caught as his hand continued its downward journey, trailing over her ribs to the indent of her waist.

He started at the bottom of her blouse, slowly unfastening her buttons.

There are all manner of things I want to see and do with you. The words played back in her mind, enticing and daunting.

This time it was she who took a step back.

"What's the matter?"

"The last time you saw me naked I was seventeen years old."

"I saw you naked last night," he reminded her.

"Not really. It was mostly dark."

"So?"

"So I'm thirty-five now."

"And I'm thirty-eight."

Nerves skittered in her tummy. "I'm trying to warn you that my body isn't what it used to be."

He stepped toward her, slid his arms around her waist. "I noticed."

She frowned. "That's not very reassuring."

He stroked his fingers up her back, tracing the column of her spine, gently drawing her nearer. "Don't you want to know what I noticed?"

"I don't think so."

He smiled. "I noticed that your breasts are a little fuller, your curves a little softer. I noticed that the body that drove me to distraction eighteen years ago is even more incredible now."

He finished unfastening her buttons but didn't immediately strip away her blouse, only parted the material enough to dip his head and press his lips to the swell of her breast.

His tongue traced the lacy edge of her bra in a lazy, leisurely caress. She felt her nipples tighten.

"Nick." It was a plea, a whimper.

"Jess."

He scraped his teeth over the aching peak. She dug her fingers into his shoulders as she felt her knees buckle. His mouth closed over her breast, suckling through the lace, and she gasped.

"And you wanted to rush through this part."

"I didn't…ahh…know about this…part."

Finally he stripped away her blouse and her skirt, then lifted her into his arms and laid her gently on top of the mattress. She waited for him to shed his clothes, impatiently craving the joining of their bodies. But he climbed onto the bed, still fully dressed, and straddled her body.

"There's more," he told her. "Much more."

Then he kissed her, a long slow kiss that seemed to last forever.

"Last night we had sex."

She smiled. "Last night we had great sex."

"Yeah," he agreed. "But tonight I'm going to show you something different."

Then his lips moved down her body, driving her to heights of passion she could never have imagined. Last night there had been heat and hunger. Tonight there was all that, and so much more.

"Tonight," he said. "I'm going to make love with you. Tonight I'm going to show you what is really between us, what keeps drawing us together even after all the time we've been apart."

"It's physical attraction," she said.

"It's that," he agreed. "And more."

She felt the sharp edge of rising panic again, fought against it. He was trying to lead her somewhere she didn't want to go, but she could choose not to follow. Keep it simple.

Except there was nothing simple about the way he was touching her, kissing her, loving her.

He opened the center clasp of her bra and parted the cups. This time when his mouth found her breast, she cried out with the shocking pleasure that speared through to her core. Then his hand slid between her legs, and with one touch, he sent her flying.

She was gasping, shuddering, as he quickly stripped away his clothes. Naked now, he settled between her thighs, his body joining intimately with hers.

"Look at me, Jessica."

She opened her eyes, blinked them into focus.

"Nick." She lifted her hips, wrapped her legs around him, glorying in the sensation of his bare skin against hers and the hard length of his arousal inside her.

Then he began to move, and she felt the need building

inside her again, pushing her higher and further, toward a spiraling peak until she shattered into a kaleidoscope of blindingly brilliant colors.

Then she heard his hoarse cry as he shattered with her.

Nick awoke the next morning feeling like the luckiest man in the world—until he reached for Jessica and realized she wasn't there.

There was, however, a note on her pillow.

Didn't want to get caught tiptoeing into the house when everyone was eating breakfast. Thanks for last night.
XO Jess

Well, the note was more than he'd got from her the first time.

Eighteen years ago, they'd spent one incredible night together, and then he'd woken up alone. Had anything really changed since then?

He wanted to believe it had.

After all, they weren't the same people they'd been back then. They were adults now. Adults with independent lives and careers in different cities, he reminded himself, which made it unlikely—if not impossible—for them to have any kind of future together.

Of course, Jess had never given any indication that she wanted a future with him. She'd been honest from the start about her plans to go back to New York. And while Manhattan wasn't on the other side of the country, it was a significant commute.

Did he want to drive two hundred miles every Friday

just to spend a couple of nights with a woman? Yes, if that woman was Jess.

But would Jess be willing to give him even that much? It seemed that she was willing to share her body, but held back from any kind of emotional intimacy. She wanted a purely physical relationship—two consenting adults engaging in no-strings sex. In the beginning, that was what Nick thought he wanted, too.

Now he wanted more.

He wanted a relationship in the fullest sense of the word. He wanted to share every part of his life with her, not just amazing sex and stolen moments.

He also knew that if he told Jessica what he wanted, she'd be on her way out of town in a New York minute. Their time was already limited enough without giving her any excuses for further limitations.

Okay, so he was going to have to take it slow if he didn't want to scare her off. But he had no intention of sneaking around as if their relationship was something to be ashamed of.

Every part of Jessica's body ached.

But she smiled, even as her muscles groaned. Because it was a good ache. The kind of ache that resulted from a quick bout of hot sweaty sex. Or an endlessly long stretch of tantalizingly slow sex. Or a lighthearted interlude of fun, playful sex. Last night, she and Nick had engaged in all of those—and more.

Eighteen years ago, her first sexual experience with Nick had been enjoyable. A sweet if not earth-shattering introduction to physical intimacy. Her recent sexual experience with Nick had been nothing short of phenomenal.

She didn't wonder whether it was age or experience that had made him such an incredible lover—she was happy just to reap the benefits.

But while the memories of last night made her body sigh contentedly, her mind was less settled. Because as wonderful as the experience had been, she sensed that something between them had changed. Something she wasn't ready to have changed.

She took her mug of coffee out onto the back porch, her concerns forgotten when she spotted Nick making his way across the yard. She smiled. "Good morning."

He didn't smile back. "I didn't think I'd have to get dressed and hike over to my sister's to hear those words."

"If you're in a lousy mood because you haven't had your coffee yet this morning, I just made a fresh pot."

"I'm not in a lousy mood," he denied. "I just want to know why you ran out in the middle of the night."

"I'll get you that coffee."

He followed her into the house.

"For your information," she said, "I left early this morning, not last night. And I kissed you goodbye and left a note."

"Okay, why didn't you stay?"

She handed him a mug of coffee. "Because although your sister probably wouldn't have any difficulty guessing where I'd spent the night, I didn't want Jake and Katie arriving at the same conclusions."

"You think they don't know?"

She opened her mouth to respond, closed it again.

"Jake caught us kissing," he reminded her.

"It's quite a leap from that to the things we were doing last night."

"Uh-huh."

"Didn't it occur to you that this—whatever *this* is that's going on between us—might be a little strange for your family?"

"Which part of that question would you like me to address first? The part about 'whatever this is' or your concern about my family?"

The thinly veiled anger in his tone warned her to tread lightly. "I think it's a little premature to be putting any kind of label on our...relationship."

He set his coffee back down. "Okay, then, let's focus on the real issue."

"Okay," she agreed hesitantly.

"I'm not going to sneak around with you, Jess."

"There's a difference between sneaking around and being discreet."

"To hell with discretion."

It was all the warning she got before he drew her into his arms and kissed her. And she kissed him back, conveniently forgetting her intention to keep their involvement a secret. At least until Kristin walked in.

"Oh. Um. Well."

Jess would have bolted to the other side of the room, except that Nick's arms remained locked around her. She tipped her head forward to lean against his chest. "It's got to be this room," she muttered. "I swear there's something about this kitchen."

"I guess this explains where you were sneaking in from at five a.m.," Kristin said.

She felt her already heated cheeks flame. So much for discretion.

But she noted that Kristin seemed a little more relaxed

this morning, with that sleepy, satisfied morning-after look indicative of having gotten more satisfaction than sleep the night before. Jess took it as a sign that Kristin and Brian's relationship was back on track.

"Is that a problem for you?" Nick asked his sister.

Kristin picked up his untouched mug of coffee and added cream. "The fact that my brother and my best friend are sleeping together?"

He nodded.

"You're both adults." Kristin sipped. "But I'd be lying if I said I didn't have concerns.

"I love both of you," she continued. "And I'm just afraid that if things don't work out, someone is going to get hurt."

"Thanks, Dear Abby," Nick said dryly.

But Jess couldn't so easily disregard Kristin's comment—she had concerns of her own. About the wisdom of getting involved with a man who'd broken her heart once before, about a relationship that obviously had no future because Nick's life was here in Pinehurst and hers was in New York.

There could be no happily-ever-after for Jessica and Nick. Not unless a fairy godmother appeared and magically eroded that geographical distance. Since that wasn't likely to happen, she knew that someone would get hurt. And Jess had a horrible feeling it would be her—because she had to go back to Manhattan, and the thought of leaving Nick again was already tearing her up inside.

Over the next few days, Nick spent as much time as possible with Jess. She continued to help out in his office, and he continued to play hooky to be with her. Everything was perfect. Or as close to perfect as it could be.

They didn't talk about the passing of time, although

there was no doubt they were both aware of it. They kept busy, trying to cram as much as possible into each twenty-four-hour period. They spent a lot of time with Kristin and Brian and the kids, but the evenings were exclusively their own.

Sometimes they made love slowly, leisurely, as if they had all the time in the world. Other times it was fast and frantic, as if they were racing against the clock. As each day blurred into the next, one thought became increasingly clear to Nick: he was in love with Jessica.

When he awoke Sunday morning with her warm, naked body tucked close to his own, it was without the usual sense of contentment. Because he knew what was coming long before she spoke the words.

"I have to go back, Nick."

He wanted to nod his head in understanding, but the truth was, he didn't understand. He didn't have the slightest clue how she could simply walk away from everything they'd shared. "Do you?"

He saw the flicker of surprise, then indecision, pass through her golden eyes. Then she nodded firmly. "Of course I do."

Now he did nod, understanding at least that he and Jess would always have different priorities.

"I've been working toward a partnership at Dawson, Murray & Neale for more than ten years. I'm not going to throw it away now."

"I'm not asking you to."

"What are you asking?"

"Just that you keep your mind open to the possibilities."

"Nick—"

"We can make this work," he said.

"Are you willing to give up your job here?" she challenged.

He'd been prepared for the question, had already considered the option. "I can't," he said. "We're already contracted for jobs well into next year."

"Then what are the possibilities?"

"We can spend our weekends together."

"Is that really what you want—two days together out of every seven?"

"It wouldn't be my first choice," he admitted. "But it's preferable to being without you."

"Wouldn't it just delay the inevitable?"

"What is it that you think is so inevitable?"

"Having to say goodbye all over again."

"I don't think that's inevitable, Jess. I don't think anything is."

She sighed. "Nick…"

He waited, wondering, hoping.

But she only pulled his head down to kiss him.

Then one kiss led to another and as their mouths melded, their bodies merged. They came together in an easy rhythm, shifting and sliding in a timeless choreography punctuated by soft sighs and quiet murmurs that built slowly to a mind-numbing and breathtaking climax.

It seemed odd to Jessica that nothing had changed.

When she got home to her apartment Sunday afternoon, she found everything exactly as she'd left it. When she got to the office Monday morning, it was the same thing. It was almost as if her life in New York had remained in limbo, waiting for her to step back into it and reassert the status quo.

But she had changed.

After only a couple of weeks back in Pinehurst, she no longer felt like she fit in.

She'd lived in New York for eighteen years now and yet whenever anyone mentioned home, she still pictured the little white bungalow with the blue shutters on Terrace Drive where she'd grown up. When she thought of the people who were important in her life, she thought of her mother, who had been living in Phoenix for the past ten years, Kristin and Brian and their kids, and, of course, Nick.

Thinking of him now, she finally accepted the truth she couldn't face in Pinehurst: she was in love. Really and truly in love for only the second time in her life. The second time with the same man.

She'd thought she loved Steve. When she'd promised to love, honor and cherish him, it was a promise she'd believed she could keep. A promise she'd intended to keep. But now, experiencing the all-encompassing love she felt for Nick all over again, she knew her promise to Steve had been a lie. She could never give her whole heart to anyone else because a part of it—the biggest part—would always belong to Nick.

She missed him.

By Friday, she was miserable. Despite his suggestion about continuing their relationship, she hadn't heard from him all week. Not even the work she'd always loved could keep her mind off of Nick. She'd said goodbye to him less than a week earlier and she already missed him unbearably.

She closed the file on her desk, noted her time in the docket, and surveyed the pile of folders on her desk still waiting to be reviewed. There was nothing that couldn't wait until Monday, but there was nothing waiting for her at home, either.

"You're probably the only person in this entire building who's still working at this hour on a Friday night."

She glanced up, her heart hammering a frantic rhythm against her ribs. Nick was standing in the doorway, one shoulder propped against the frame, that slow, sexy smile curving his lips.

Her fingers gripped the edge of the desk, holding her in place so she didn't jump up and throw herself into his arms. She forced herself to respond casually, "Ed Murray's still here."

"Tall man with curly gray hair and little round glasses?"

She nodded.

"He was leaving as I came in."

"What are you doing here, Nick? Are you in need of some legal advice?"

"No." He finally stepped into her office, his hands behind his back. "But I do need a lawyer."

"What kind of lawyer?"

"You."

Her lips curved in spite of herself. "You always did have the good lines. Which one did you use to get past security?"

"I didn't need a line—I had these." He brought his arm from behind his back and handed her a bouquet of flowers— a huge arrangement of blooms in dazzling autumn colors.

"They're beautiful." She stood up to take them from him and couldn't resist the impulse to bury her face in the blooms and inhale the fragrant perfume.

"Turns out your security guy is a romantic at heart," he said. "Of course, I had to show photo ID and sign my name in blood, but he let me preserve the element of surprise by not buzzing up to announce my arrival."

"But why are you really here?"

"I heard about this great new restaurant that recently opened on 49th Street. I made reservations for eight o'clock."

"You drove two hundred miles to go out for dinner?"

"Nah. I drove two hundred miles because I've missed you like crazy this week."

Her heart sighed. "I missed you, too, but—"

Apparently he wasn't interested in hearing any qualifiers, because his lips were already moving over hers in a masterful and irresistible seduction.

She'd told herself it was over. She'd been miserable all week, believing it was over, believing she'd done the right thing in ending their fledgling relationship before coming back to the city. And now he was here.

She should have been annoyed that he'd disregarded everything she'd said. Instead, she was only grateful.

"Maybe we could continue this…conversation at my apartment," she suggested.

"We should go for dinner first."

"We can have dinner later."

He shook his head. "I promise you that when we get to your place and I get you naked, it will be at least thirty-six hours before either of us even thinks about going anywhere else. And since I skipped lunch today to leave work early, I really need to fuel up before that."

"Thirty-six hours?"

"Jess," he warned.

"Don't you remember me telling you about all the great restaurants in this city that deliver?" She smiled. "Only one of us would need to be dressed to answer the door."

"I'll cancel our reservation."

* * *

He didn't keep her naked for the entire thirty-six hours. Sometime late Saturday afternoon, they got dressed, took a walk through Central Park, kissed in front of Cleopatra's Needle, ate hot dogs from a street vendor, rode on the carousel, kissed by the reservoir, then went back to her apartment and got naked once more.

It seemed that even when they'd just finished making love, he couldn't stop wanting her all over again. He'd never felt this kind of urgency—except for one night eighteen years earlier. He'd been desperate with wanting her, needing to touch her, possess her.

Afterward, he'd blamed his youth, his hormones. But he was thirty-eight now, and there was still something about Jessica that called to him on a primal level.

She was his.

She'd always been his.

From that first night so many years ago, she'd been branded by his touch. It didn't matter how many men might have passed through her life in the intervening years, how many women might have passed through his, all that mattered was that she was back in his arms again.

And this time, he didn't intend to let her go.

The more difficult task, he realized, would be convincing Jessica that they were meant to be together long-term.

Jess didn't want to think about the future. She didn't want to imagine a time when she and Nick couldn't be together exactly like this. They'd spent an incredible couple of days together, but again she knew it was only an interlude in her life. And as much as she hated to be the one to bring it to an end, there were things they needed to talk about. Things she should have told Nick before they'd ever got involved again.

But it wasn't until they were finishing up dinner Sunday night that she finally broached the subject.

"Last weekend, when we made love the last time before I left your place, we didn't use birth control."

"I realized that after you'd gone." He picked up the wine bottle to refill her glass, then his own. "Do you want me to say I'm sorry?"

"Are you?"

He set the bottle back down. "I'm sorry we didn't talk about it first, that it was an oversight rather than a conscious decision. Or maybe it was a conscious decision on my part," he admitted. "Because truthfully, I wouldn't be sorry if you got pregnant."

"I *can't* get pregnant, Nick."

He frowned. "Then why have we been using condoms?"

"Aside from the obvious answer that it's smart to practice safe sex, because I didn't want to explain why we didn't need to worry about birth control." But she knew she couldn't avoid it any longer. "When my appendix ruptured and I lost the baby, there were complications. Scarring."

She took a bracing sip of the merlot. This was a conversation they should have had weeks ago, before they'd ever got involved again. But she hadn't believed it would go this far, that Nick would have any expectation of pursuing their relationship after she left Pinehurst.

"I didn't really know about it until Steve and I got married and I had trouble conceiving." She traced a finger around the base of her glass. "My doctor sent me for some tests and found that one of my fallopian tubes is completely blocked off."

"Oh."

She didn't need to look at him to see his disappointment. It was all in that single word.

"She said I might be able to conceive through the other tube, but two years of good old-fashioned trying proved otherwise."

"She didn't offer any other options?"

"I could have had surgery," she admitted. "I had even booked an appointment to have the procedure done, but then Steve and I split up and there wasn't any reason to go through with it."

He paused a moment before asking, "Would you have the surgery now?"

She was prepared for the question. She knew how important it was to Nick to have a family, but it didn't change what her answer would be.

She shook her head. "I'm almost thirty-six years old, Nick. Even if I had the surgery, even if it was successful, I don't know that I want a baby at this point in my life."

"Oh."

She could tell he was surprised by her response—and again disappointed. But she couldn't let their relationship continue under the false assumption that they would some-day have the family he wanted so much.

She pushed her plate aside. "I should have told you sooner."

He nodded.

"I know you were planning to stay until morning, but I understand if you want to leave tonight."

There was a heavy pause before he finally said, "I'm try-ing to figure out which one of us should be more insulted by that comment."

"I didn't mean—"

"You don't usually say things you don't mean," he in-terrupted. "Do you really believe that I would throw away everything else that's between us because you can't have children?"

She pushed away from the table, started to clear away the dishes. "I know how much you want a family."

Nick followed her into the kitchen. "And you expected that I would walk out on you because of something that happened when you were pregnant with my baby eighteen years ago?"

"This didn't happen because I was pregnant," she told him. "It happened because my appendix ruptured."

"But—"

"No. You're not responsible for this, Nick." She turned away from him to load the plates into the dishwasher. "And I don't want you to be with me because you have some misplaced sense of guilt."

"What if I want to be with you because I love you?"

Her eyes filled with tears. "Don't tell me that, not now."

"Do you think I just came up with it on the spur of the moment?"

"I don't know."

"It wasn't how I'd planned to tell you, Jess, but I was certain of my feelings before I came down here this weekend."

"What I told you tonight has to change things."

"It doesn't change how I feel about you," he said. "And I'm not going anywhere tonight."

Chapter Fifteen

Jess woke up earlier than usual Monday morning after a restless night. Nick had to leave to go back to Pinehurst, but she didn't want him to leave with so many things still unresolved between them and she had no idea how to resolve them.

She usually didn't have time for anything more than a granola bar or cup of yogurt before heading to the office. But since she hadn't been able to sleep, she figured she might as well cook breakfast. She was breaking eggs into a bowl when Nick came into the kitchen, freshly showered and shaved.

She breathed in the clean scent of his aftershave as he bent to kiss her and felt an irrational urge to cry. Instead she forced a smile. "Hungry?"

"She's sexy, smart, and she cooks. I feel like I must have died and gone to heaven."

"Fried or scrambled?" she asked, ignoring his comment.

"Scrambled."

She added milk to the bowl and began mixing as Nick helped himself to coffee.

"You're not going to ask me to come back next weekend, are you?"

She wanted to—and it was because she wanted to that she knew she couldn't. She shook her head as she moved the eggs around the pan. "It won't work."

"Why not?"

Dammit, why couldn't he just accept that she was trying to do the right thing? Why was he making this so hard for both of them?

She grabbed a plate from the cupboard, dumped the eggs onto it. "I can't give you what you want."

"Because you can't have a baby?"

She flinched at the bluntness of the question. But now that she'd told him, there was no need to tiptoe around the reality of the situation. "Yes."

"There are other options if we really want children," he pointed out. "But having a family doesn't matter to me as much as being with you."

"Okay, aside from the issue of children, there is another—and bigger—problem." She took the bacon from the microwave, added a few slices to his plate along with the toast she'd just buttered, and set his breakfast on the table. "Our lives are in different cities, Nick."

He sat down, considering her argument. "That's only an obstacle if you let it be."

"Two hundred miles *is* an obstacle, regardless of my feelings about it."

"You wouldn't have any difficulty getting a job in Pinehurst."

She sat down across from him with her plate of toast and her coffee. "Last week you said you wouldn't ask me to give up my chance at a partnership."

"And I wouldn't be asking now except that you told Kristin you were thinking of moving on."

She should have known that little piece of information would somehow get back to Nick. But she hadn't meant it, not really. She'd simply been talking out loud, and while it was true that she did feel stifled at Dawson, Murray & Neale at times, she couldn't imagine being anywhere else.

"Moving on as in *expanding* my clientele, not downsizing it."

He pushed away from the table to refill his mug with coffee, shaking his head as he did so. "You're determined not to compromise."

"You're not asking me to compromise," she protested. "You're asking me to sacrifice a career I've spent the better part of ten years building."

"Okay. If you won't move back to Pinehurst, I'll come here."

She laughed, then noted the expression on his face. "You're serious."

"Yeah."

"You told me you couldn't."

He shrugged. "It would require some serious juggling, but it might work."

"No."

"Why not?"

"Because you hate it here."

He shrugged. "Hate is a rather strong word."

"I know, and I distinctly remember you saying 'I hate New York City.'"

"That was before."

"Before what?"

"Before I realized that I want to get married and spend the rest of my life with you."

She set down her unfinished toast, wiped her fingers on a napkin. "This is kind of abrupt."

"It's taken eighteen years for us to get to this point— I'd hardly say that's abrupt."

"We've both been married before," she pointed out.

"Don't compare what we have now with the mistakes we made in the past."

"Did you think it was a mistake when you married Tina?"

He thought about the question for a long minute. "No," he admitted. "I wouldn't have married her if I hadn't thought we could make it work. But I always knew that what I felt for her didn't compare to the feelings I had for you.

"There have been other women in my life—before and after that first night we spent together. But nothing I've ever felt for anyone else compared to what I feel for you. What I've always felt for you."

"We want different things, Nick. Getting married won't change that."

"I think we both want the same thing," he said. "You're just afraid to admit it."

There were times, she realized, that it was a definite disadvantage to be with a man who knew her so well.

"I think you need to give yourself some time to think about this," she said. "I think we both need time to think about this."

"How much time?" he asked, frustration evident in his

tone. "How long am I going to have to wait before you'll believe that I want to spend my life with you?"

It was a hypothetical question, and yet it offered a workable solution to the situation. "Six months."

"What?"

She nodded. The more she thought about it, the more sense it made. It was the opportunity for a break—a way to avoid the messy breakup she'd feared. A dignified exit from a relationship that would otherwise only end up hurting both of them.

"Six months," she said again. "If, after that time has passed, you still want a future with me, we'll try to work something out."

"I've loved you for eighteen *years,* Jess. Do you really think that's going to change in six months?"

"If you're so sure it won't, then waiting six months shouldn't be a problem."

"I don't want to wait."

"Please, Nick. It's been an emotional few weeks for both of us. I just want to make sure we're doing the right thing."

"And what are we supposed to do during the next six months?"

Though her stomach was twisted into all kinds of knots, she forced herself to take a sip of her coffee. "I don't think we should see each other."

"Why not?"

"Because our physical relationship will only complicate the situation." She stood up to carry her plate and mug to the sink.

"I'm not buying any of this, Jess."

She shrugged.

"If that's really your concern, we could continue to spend time together but not have sex."

Yeah—that was likely.

"I need to be on my own to be able to think about this objectively," she insisted.

"And you think you'll have a better handle on this in six months if I leave you alone during that time?"

"We both will."

"No." He pushed away from the table, dumped his dishes beside hers. "You're thinking I'll either get frustrated or bored before then and move on with my life without you. Or maybe you're expecting that this conversation will piss me off so much I'll storm out now and the next six months will be irrelevant."

She lifted her chin. "I'm just asking for some time. You're free to interpret that however you like."

He just stood there, staring at her for a long moment. She forced herself to hold his gaze, determined not to reveal the slightest hint of weakness or uncertainty.

Nick took a step toward her, laid his hand against her cheek. "It's hard to let go of someone you love," he said softly. "Sometimes it's even harder to ask them to stay."

Then he kissed her, just the briefest touch of his lips to hers. "Goodbye, Jessica."

It had been her idea. And yet, as Jessica watched Nick's SUV turn at the corner and disappear from sight, she was helpless to stop the tears. In a short time, he'd become an integral part of her life again. Now she'd severed that part—finally and completely. And she couldn't believe how much it hurt.

She didn't want to live her life without him, but she

couldn't give him what he wanted. Despite what he said about not needing to have a family, she'd seen the look in his eyes when she'd told him she couldn't have children: shock, despair. Then the spark of hope when she'd mentioned surgery. A spark she'd extinguished by refusing to consider the option.

She just couldn't imagine going through with it now—not at this stage in her life. If she'd had the procedure five years earlier and believed there was even a chance she could have Nick's baby...

She shook her head. She'd spent too many years thinking how things might have been different if only she'd chosen a different course. It was time to finally accept the way things were and live the life she'd built for herself.

She wiped the tears from her eyes, touched up her make-up, and went in to work.

Jess had intended to wait another week to call Kristin. She needed some time to come to terms with the end of her relationship with Nick before she could answer the questions she knew his sister would have.

But Thursday night, Kristin called her.

"Caleb has chicken pox," she said, and then she laughed. "He's miserable and covered in spots, and I can't help being ecstatic because it's such a normal kid thing."

Jess chuckled. "I guess this means that life is back on track for all of you?"

"I think our lives jumped the track with Caleb's accident, but we've learned to go in new directions. In fact," she said, "I'm going back to school in the new year."

"That's terrific."

"Brian brought home a college course calendar yesterday," Kristin explained. "I'm not sure that I'll actually work toward a certificate, but there are several courses that seem interesting."

"I'm really happy for you."

"My life is good," Kristin agreed. "Now if only I could do something about my brother."

It was an obvious trap, but one Jessica couldn't help but step into. "Is everything okay with Nick?"

"That's a strange question coming from the woman who dumped him."

"I didn't dump him."

Kristin's silence was telling.

Jess sighed. "Okay, I dumped him. But you know it wouldn't have worked out between us."

"I know that a good friend once told me love is worth fighting for."

"That's when I was talking about you and Brian."

"What makes this different?"

"Everything."

Kristin sighed. "I didn't call to get on your case about Nick," she said. "I actually called to invite you for Thanksgiving."

"I can't—"

"If you come, there will be ten," Kristin interrupted. "And I can seat you at the opposite end of the table so you won't even have to talk to my brother if you don't want to."

"I appreciate the invitation," she said. "But I really do have plans already. My mom always comes up to New York for the weekend, for the Macy's parade and Christmas shopping."

"What about Christmas, then?"

Jess hesitated but went with her instincts. "I promise to make the trip some time over the holidays," she said, hoping by then her heart might have started healing.

"Mom invited Jessica to come for Thanksgiving."

Nick continued peeling carrots, as if Katie's statement hadn't triggered a dozen questions in his mind.

"Don't you want to know if she's coming?"

"Aren't you supposed to be chopping these carrots?"

"She's not," his niece told him.

He wasn't surprised by her response—or by the sharp disappointment he felt.

She huffed out an impatient breath. "I'm trying to have a conversation here."

"You seem to be managing quite well on your own."

"Do you love her?"

"How is that any of your business?"

She tilted her head, looking at him with the wisdom of a woman well beyond her fifteen years.

"Okay, yes," he said at last.

"Then why are you here when she's in New York?"

"Because, Miss Nosey, that's how Jessica wants it."

She shook her head. "If you believe that, then you don't know anything about her."

"And what do you know about it?" he challenged.

"I know that she was in love with you a long time ago and you screwed it up."

"Where the hel—heck did you get that information?"

"Not from Jessica," Katie said loyally. "She only told me that things didn't work out. I read between the lines."

"Typical woman," he muttered.

She smiled, apparently pleased by his comment.

"Jessica and I spent a lot of time together when Caleb was in the hospital—we bonded."

"Apparently."

She dumped the carrots into a glass bowl. "If you really love her, you need to go after her."

"I did," he said, somewhat baffled to realize he was discussing his personal life with his teenage niece. "She sent me away."

Katie rolled her eyes. "Because she wants to know that you think she's worth fighting for."

Nick was updating his résumé when the phone rang. It was a welcome interruption, as he was beginning to seriously doubt the prospects of any New York architectural firm hiring a thirty-eight-year-old whose experience was limited to the design and renovation of residential homes and local businesses in small-town Pinehurst.

But he wasn't going to give up without giving it his best shot. This time, he was going to prove he could be every bit as stubborn as Jessica. This time, he wasn't going to let her get away.

"Nick, it's Tina." Her voice practically hummed with excitement. "I have terrific news."

"I could use some right about now." It had been nine weeks since he'd seen Jessica, and he was starting to have serious doubts about the decisions he'd made.

"I got a call today from an out-of-town buyer looking for a house in Pinehurst, something close to the local schools, with a big backyard and a home office. She said something about relocating for her husband's job and when I described your house to her, she thought it sounded perfect."

"My house? But it isn't even officially listed yet."

"That's only because we haven't had a chance to hammer out the details with respect to closing date and asking price."

Nick felt a brief spurt of panic as he thought about the house he'd taken such care in planning and building. He looked out the window, at the fringe of trees at the back of the property, and thought of the creek beyond them.

When he and Kristin had decided to split the property, he'd insisted that the division be made so that the creek would be part of his land. Even then, he'd been unable to let go of the memories it held—memories of the times he'd spent there with Jessica.

"Nick? You do still want to sell, don't you?"

He forgot about the house and the land and thought of Jessica, and her continued insistence that her life was in Manhattan.

"Of course, it's okay if you've changed your mind," Tina continued. "But I thought—"

"No," he interrupted. "I haven't changed my mind. I want to sell."

"Great."

He heard the relief in her voice.

"The buyer was going to try to come down this weekend," she continued. "Could I bring her by to see the place Friday afternoon?"

The cleaning lady would be in that morning, so Friday afternoon was probably as good a time as any. "Sure. If I'm not here, I'll leave a key in the mailbox."

"I'd really like you to be there," Tina said, "if you can. In case she has any questions."

Normally it would be the real estate agent's job to answer the questions, but as he hadn't yet had an opportunity to discuss details with Tina, he could see her point. "Okay."

"Great, I'll see you Friday afternoon around four."

As luck would have it, Nick got tied up with an electrical inspection at a construction site Friday afternoon and it was almost four-thirty by the time he pulled into his driveway.

Tina's car, he noted, was still parked on the street in front of the house. She met him at the door with a smile. "You made it."

"Sorry, I'm late."

"Not a problem," she assured him. "But I do have another client waiting. Do you mind finishing the tour?"

"No, I guess not."

She smiled, then lowered her voice conspiratorially. "Your potential purchaser seems very impressed with the house and the property. She's upstairs checking out the bedrooms now, and I can tell you she absolutely loved the hot tub."

So had Jess, he remembered.

And then he looked up, and there she was.

He blinked, certain he was imagining her. But when he opened his eyes again, she was still standing at the top of the stairs. She was dressed as if she'd come from work, in a fitted jacket and knee-length skirt. The cut of the suit was conservative, the color—a vibrant shade of red—was not.

Her smile was hesitant. "Hello, Nick."

"Jessica."

Tina cleared her throat. "I really do have to run."

"Sure," Nick managed.

"Thanks, Tina," Jess said.

With a wave and a smile, his ex-wife was gone, and he and Jess were alone.

She came down the stairs, her fingers trailing over the bleached oak banister.

"Are you looking to buy a house?" he asked.

"Actually, I am."

"In Pinehurst?"

"Real estate in Manhattan is out of my price range."

She moved past him and into the kitchen. "I love this room. It's so big and bright." She turned to face him. "Why are you selling?"

"I was planning to relocate."

"Was?"

"I guess that depends on you—what you're really doing here."

"Kristin told me you've been looking for someone to take over your part of the business," she said, sidestepping his inquiry. "Why didn't you tell me?"

"I would have," he said. "At the end of this ridiculous six-month hiatus you insisted upon."

"You love your work here."

"I love you more."

He saw her eyes fill with tears before she turned away. She moved to the bay window overlooking the backyard. "You've made a beautiful home here, Nick."

"It's only a house."

"I can picture a swing set and sandbox in the backyard, one of those little wading pools under the big maple tree, toys scattered over the deck." She turned to him. "Can you picture it, Nick?"

All too clearly. It was a house created with dreams of a family—his family. But he'd let go of those dreams because the picture faded without Jessica in it.

"I wanted to do the right thing—to let you go so you could be with someone who could give you the family you deserve."

He noticed that she'd used the past tense and let himself hope.

"I love *you*," he said again.

"Despite the ridiculous six-month hiatus I imposed?"

He finally smiled. "Yeah, despite that."

"You know that I love you, too?"

"I was hoping that's why you're here."

"I do love you, Nick."

They were the words he'd waited a long time to hear, words that made him want to take her in his arms and kiss her until the endless weeks they'd spent apart were forgotten. Instead he leaned back against the counter and tucked his hands into his pockets.

Her teeth sank into her bottom lip. "I was thinking that this might be an appropriate time for you to kiss me."

"If I touch you now, I won't be able to stop, and there are still things we need to talk about."

She breached the distance that separated them. "We can talk later."

It was much later before they resumed their conversation.

Jessica was lying naked in his arms, her head cradled against his shoulder, her body luxuriously warm and sated.

"I missed you, Nick."

"I knew you wouldn't last six months."

She heard the smug arrogance in his tone, propped herself up on an elbow to look down at him. "You did, huh?"

He smiled. "Well, I hoped you wouldn't."

"Did Tina tell you why I wanted to buy your house?"

"I forgot Tina was even in the room when I saw you standing at the top of the stairs," he admitted.

Now it was her turn to smile. "I told her I was relocating for my husband's job," she reminded him. "So unless you want me to be called a liar, you're going to have to marry me."

He brushed a lock of hair from her cheek, tucked it behind her ear. "Have to, huh?"

"Well, it's really your call."

"No—it's always been yours." He cupped the back of her head and brought her mouth down to his, kissed her softly. "I missed you, Jess."

"I missed you, too." She kissed him again, longer, deeper this time. "But before we get distracted again, there is something else we need to talk about."

"What's that?"

"A few weeks ago, I went to see my doctor. To talk about having the surgery."

"You don't have to do that, Jess. As long as I have you, I have everything I've ever wanted."

She wondered how it was that he always seemed to know the exact right thing to say to her. "Well, you're going to get more than you wanted then."

He stilled. "You had the surgery?"

She shook her head. "As it turns out, I didn't need to. Apparently I *can* get pregnant the old-fashioned way."

Nick was stunned. "But…"

She understood his confusion. She'd been as stunned as he was by the news. After years of failing to conceive with her ex-husband, it seemed impossible that one night with Nick could have produced such different results. "Even my doctor couldn't explain it," she admitted. "Maybe there isn't an explanation, except that the chemistry was finally right."

His eyes widened as his hand went automatically to her still flat tummy. "You're really…pregnant?"

"Almost three months."

"We're going to have a baby?"

She smiled. "Yeah."

He swallowed. "Are you okay with this?"

She knew he was remembering what she'd said about not wanting a baby at this stage in her life. "I didn't want to go through the uncertainty of surgery, the disappointment of trying—and failing—to conceive. But I want this baby, Nick. *Our* baby."

"Our baby," he echoed, then grinned. "Wow."

"Yeah, it takes a while to get your mind around it, doesn't it?"

"I'm sure I'll manage."

"You've got a few months yet to get used to the idea," she told him. "But if everything goes according to schedule, you'll be a daddy before the end of June."

He kissed her softly, deeply. "Maybe we could try to fit in 'husband' before then?"

"We can try," she agreed. "But things are going to be pretty chaotic with the move and the new job."

"Tina told me she expects the house should sell quickly and—"

"I told Tina your house is off the market."

"Why?"

"Because I can't imagine a more wonderful place for our child to grow up than in this house, in this town. Close to his aunt and uncle and cousins."

"It'll be a hell of a commute to your office."

"Not to my new office. I had an interview today at Grayson & Associates. I start after the holidays."

"What about your partnership at Dawson, Murray & Neale?"

"It was offered to me a couple of weeks ago," she admitted. "The bigger office, my name on the door, more money—everything I'd wanted for so long. And then there was the mention of overseas travel, additional social obligations and even longer hours, and I realized it wasn't the right choice for me.

"How was I ever supposed to achieve any kind of balance in my life if my job took everything out of me? Where would I find the time to be with you if I was always at the office?"

"Are you saying that you turned it down?"

She smiled. "You sound almost as surprised as Mr. Dawson."

"You've wanted that partnership for ten years."

"I've wanted you for eighteen." She ran her hand over his chest, felt the strong, steady beat of his heart beneath her palm. "So are you going to offer me a partnership—or have you changed your mind?"

"I think a partnership would work." He twined his fingers with hers, then tugged her off balance so she tumbled down on top of him. "Did you want to negotiate contractual terms?"

"The only term I'm concerned about is the duration."

"Forever."

She smiled and wrapped her arms around him. "That's what I wanted to hear."

* * * * *

Don't miss Brenda Harlen's thrilling new novel
DANGEROUS PASSIONS
coming next month to Silhouette Intimate Moments.
Available wherever Silhouette Books are sold.

Coming in November from

INTIMATE MOMENTS™

and author

Brenda Harlen
Dangerous Passions
IM #1394

With a hit man coming after her,
beautiful Shannon Vaughn was forced to
go on the run with Michael Courtland,
the sexy P.I. assigned to protect her. But
as the enemy closed in, Shannon realized
she was in greater danger
of losing her heart....

*Don't miss this exciting story...
only from Silhouette Books.*

Available at your favorite retail outlet.

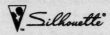

SPECIAL EDITION™

presents

the first book in a heartwarming new series by

Kristin Hardy

Because there's
no place like home
for the holidays…

WHERE THERE'S SMOKE

(November 2005, SE#1720)

Sloane Hillyard took a very personal interest in her work inventing fire safety equipment—after all, her firefighter brother had died in the line of duty. And when Boston fire captain Nick Trask signed up to test her inventions, things got even more personal… their mutual attraction set off alarms. But could Sloane trust her heart to a man who risked his life and limb day in and day out?

Available November 2005 at your favorite retail outlet.

Where love comes alive™

COMING NEXT MONTH

#1717 THE BORROWED RING—Gina Wilkins
Family Found
Tracking down childhood friend Daniel Andreas was an assignment close to P.I. Brittany Samples's heart. But things took an unexpected turn when "B.J." caught her quarry—who dispensed with reunion formalities and recruited her to pose as his wife! Soon their dangerous new mission had B.J. wishing the husband-and-wife cover wasn't just an act....

#1718 A MONTANA HOMECOMING—Allison Leigh
When Laurel Runyan returned to Lucius, Montana, after her estranged father's death, she had nowhere else to go—she'd recently broken off an engagement and given up her job and apartment. But having her first love, sheriff Shane Golightly, as a neighbor reopened old wounds. Was Laurel ready to give her hometown—and Shane—a second chance?

#1719 SECRETS OF A GOOD GIRL—Jen Safrey
Most Likely To...
While at Saunders University, coed Cassidy Maxwell and teaching assistant Eric Barnes had put off romance until Cassidy got her degree. Then she hadn't shown up at graduation, and Eric was crushed. Now, years later, he'd gone to London to woo her back. But Cassidy wanted to keep her childhood friend—and her own dark Saunders secrets—in the past....

#1720 WHERE THERE'S SMOKE—Kristin Hardy
Holiday Hearts
After her brother died fighting a blaze, Sloane Hillyard took action, inventing a monitor to improve firefighter safety. She found a reluctant test subject in Boston fire captain Nick Trask—who warmed to the task as his attraction for Sloane grew. But after losing her brother, would Sloane risk her heart on another of Boston's bravest?

#1721 MARRIAGE, INTERRUPTED—Karen Templeton
Cass Stern was on edge—newly widowed, saddled with debt, running a business and *very* pregnant. Things couldn't get weirder—until her first husband, Blake Carter, showed up at her second husband's funeral. Blake wanted more time with their teenaged son—and he wanted Cass back. Cass's body screamed "Yes!" but...well, there were a lot of buts....

#1722 WHERE HE BELONGS—Gail Barrett
For Harley-riding, smoke-jumping rebel Wade Winslow, it was tough going back to Millstown and facing his past. But former flame Erin McCuen and her financial troubles struck a chord with the bad boy, so he decided to stay for a while. The stubborn and independent woman wouldn't accept Wade's help...but could she convince him to give their renewed passion a fighting chance?